RACING THE WIND

'I'm sorry,' Gina said quietly. 'But I won't let Jody risk her life.'

Jody opened her mouth to protest.

But before she could say anything, Juan moved close to Gina and spoke to her urgently. '*Señora* McGrath,' he said, 'I promise. I will look after Jody. She will be safe with me . . .'

Gina nodded. She bit her lip and looked at Leon. 'Do you really think this will work?'

'I don't know,' Leon replied honestly. 'But we have to try.' He started up the motor and guided the boat slowly and carefully towards the sandbank. 'We're Posy's only hope of survival.'

Look out for more titles in this series

1: Into the Blue
2: Touching the Waves
3: Riding the Storm
4: Under the Stars
5: Chasing the Dream

Dolphin Diaries™

RACING THE WIND

Lucy Daniels

Hodder Children's Books

a division of Hodder Headline Limited

Special thanks to Lisa Tuttle

Thanks also to the Whale and Dolphin Conservation Society for reviewing the information contained in this book

First published in Great Britain in 2001
by Hodder Children's Books

10 9 8 7 6 5 4 3 2 1

A Catalogue record for this book is available from the British Library

ISBN 0 340 78497 0

Typeset by Avon Dataset Ltd, Bidford-on-Avon, Warks

Printed and bound in Great Britain by
Clays Ltd, St Ives plc

Hodder Children's Books
a division of Hodder Headline
338 Euston Road
London NW1 3BH

1

October 31 – morning – the Caribbean.

Just saw a pod of orcas – I counted twenty-five of them as they came right up to the side of our boat. They were absolutely gorgeous, and very playful and friendly, too. Even though they're called 'killer whales,' they're really dolphins – the biggest of them all!

Just remembered – it's Hallowe'en! How weird to think that Lindsay and Maria and all my other friends back in Florida will be dressing up and going out trick-or-treating tonight – while I'm in the middle of the Caribbean, on my way to Venezuela!

The past few weeks have been so great – we've

spotted many different species of dolphin. Mom and Dad got most of them on video, too

Jody McGrath paused and gazed over the side of *Dolphin Dreamer*, hoping to spot more orcas.

She had been travelling with the project known as Dolphin Universe for a few months now. Her parents, Craig and Gina McGrath, were marine biologists. They headed the project, sailing around the world with their family and crew to study dolphins.

But the orcas were long gone, and Jody couldn't see any sign of life above the small, choppy waves. With a sigh, she turned back to her diary.

We've been really lucky with the weather, too. Plenty of wind, not too much rain. No storms at all. But Harry doesn't seem too pleased with the wind today, for some reason . . . he called it a 'backing wind' and it seems to worry him . . .

Jody broke off again to look towards the helm where their captain, Harry Pierce, was steering.

Just then, the first mate, Cameron Tucker, came

out of the radio room, a worried expression on his handsome face. 'Captain,' he said, 'I've been listening to the weather reports, and they're not good . . .'

'That tropical depression?' Harry responded quickly.

Cam nodded. 'It's been upgraded. They're calling it a hurricane now. Hurricane Delilah.'

Jody caught her breath, shocked. They were going to get caught in a *hurricane*?

Gina McGrath frowned and pushed an unruly lock of black hair out of her face as she spoke. 'But surely it's awfully late for a hurricane . . ?'

Harry nodded agreement. 'The worst months are August and September. But hurricanes have been known to happen as late as November. We've had luck on our side all summer – but our luck may just have run out,' he concluded, his bearded face very grim.

'Should we put into port somewhere?' Craig McGrath asked, stepping forward and putting an arm around his wife.

But Harry shook his head. 'Too late for that now,' he replied. 'If we head towards any of the islands in the Lesser Antilles, we'd be sailing straight into the hurricane's path. That's the most dangerous route of all.' He gazed out at the deceptively calm-looking sea and drew a deep breath.

Turning back to Craig and Gina he said decisively, 'Our safest course is to keep south of Delilah's path. Wherever that takes us. I hope we can keep out of her way. But if she catches up with us . . . well, hurricanes rotate clockwise, so if we stand with our back to the eye and keep heading to our left, hopefully we'll be spun off by the incoming high winds.'

Cam nodded in agreement. 'It won't be a comfortable ride, though,' he added, glancing at the McGraths.

Gina managed a rather wan smile. 'Maybe I'd better pass out the seasickness tablets,' she said, trying to joke.

'Sounds like a good idea,' Harry replied seriously. He turned to Craig. 'Would you take the helm? I need to get below and plot a new course. Give me a shout at the first sign of a change in the weather.' Glancing at the horizon, where grey clouds were massing, he added, 'I think we've got a couple of hours yet.'

Jody's heart was pounding. She couldn't help feeling very afraid. Growing up in Florida, she'd seen the damage a hurricane could do. This was much more scary than trick-or-treat . . .

Seeing Jody's face, Gina hugged her briefly. 'Honey, why don't you go down and make sure everything in your cabin is safely stowed away?' she said. 'Tell Brittany and your brothers to do the same. We don't want things flying around and causing problems when the weather gets rough.'

Jody nodded and went below to find her eight-year-old twin brothers, Sean and Jimmy.

They had already heard the news.

'We're going to help Mei Lin check on the bilge pumps,' Jimmy told her. Mei Lin Zhong, a slender young Chinese woman, was the engineer and cook.

'It's very important that the pumps are working right,' Sean added. 'Otherwise when the giant waves start crashing down on us the boat would fill up with water and we'd sink!' His blue eyes sparkled with excitement. 'Did you know that in a really big storm, waves can be as tall as buildings? Fifty feet high – or even more!'

Jody shuddered and hurried back to the cabin she

shared with Brittany Pierce, the captain's thirteen-year-old daughter.

Brittany was stretched out in her bunk, listening to music through the earphones of her portable CD player. She sat up when she saw Jody's worried expression. 'What's wrong?' she asked.

The colour drained from her face when she heard Jody's news. 'A hurricane!' she cried. 'Oh, what are we going to do?'

'Your dad thinks we can outrun it,' Jody explained. 'But it could be a rough ride . . .'

Breaking the bad news to Brittany

'Oh, *why* didn't my mother take me with her to Paris instead of leaving me with Daddy?' Brittany cried. 'She'll be sorry when she hears how I drowned!'

'Nobody's going to drown!' Jody replied sharply. 'Harry's taken us through storms before, and he'll get us through this one, too.' She spoke with more certainty than she felt. She didn't want Brittany to know that she was frightened, too.

There was a knock at the cabin door, then Maddie looked in. The attractive young black woman was the McGraths' personal assistant and also the on-board teacher, making sure that Jody, Brittany and the twins didn't fall behind in their studies while they were away from their regular schools.

'It's time for lessons, girls,' she said. 'I'm used to having to round up the boys, but it's not like you two to be late!'

'But there's a hurricane coming!' Brittany cried.

Maddie nodded. 'I know, honey,' she said quietly. 'It worries me, too. But fretting about it won't help. We need to keep our minds occupied – and I think history, geography and math are the best things for that, while Harry and Cam concentrate on sailing us out of danger.'

* * *

The storm struck suddenly, mid-afternoon.

Even though they'd all been waiting for it, the fury of the sea was a shock, and seemed to come out of nowhere.

Dolphin Dreamer pitched and rocked like a wild fairground ride. Despite the seasickness tablet her mother had given her, Jody felt her stomach lurch queasily. Nervously, she asked her father if it was safe to sail through such a storm.

Craig nodded. 'The eye of the hurricane is still many miles away,' he explained. 'These winds are strong . . . but not deadly. Not yet. And Harry reckons he can *use* their power – to get us *away* from the eye of the hurricane.' He smiled at her and said softly, 'Harry knows what he's doing, honey. He's one of the very best.'

The winds raged and blew on into the night. Under Harry and Cam's skilful guidance, *Dolphin Dreamer* flew on ahead of the hurricane, travelling ever farther south.

No one had much appetite for dinner, and they all went early to bed.

Lying curled up in her bunk, listening to the raging wind and the waves that lashed against the hull, Jody thought she would never manage to sleep. But sleep must have overtaken her eventually, because when she next opened her eyes, everything was peaceful and calm, and there was the brilliant gleam of sunlight through the porthole.

November 1 – morning – the Caribbean
We made it!

Hurricane Delilah is still charging northwards, towards the Dominican Republic – but we're safely far south of any danger from her. The sun is shining, the sky is blue and clear, and everybody is in a great mood. Even Brittany, reminded that her dad is a hero, is as proud as if she was the one who'd sailed us to safety! The way she talks, you'd think she was never scared for even a second! She says she always knew her dad could do it . . .

As for Harry – he's gone to bed, not to be disturbed all day! Dad and Mom are taking turns at the helm.

Our next stop will be the island of Trinidad, so we can stock up on fuel. Then it's Venezuela, where we'll head inland to see some river dolphins!

* * *

The next few days were smooth sailing for *Dolphin Dreamer*. But once they left the Atlantic Ocean and entered the wide, brown Orinoco River delta, the wind died away. The air was like a thick, hot blanket. To make any progress at all, Harry had to use the engine constantly.

November 7 – morning – Ciudad Guyana, Venezuela
We're here!

After being out at sea for so long, it was really weird to wake up this morning to all the noises of a city – traffic, horns, sirens, people's voices shouting, some kind of heavy machinery, even music. And the smells! *Motor oil, exhausts, garbage, frying food – and I don't know what else.*

We're berthed in a noisy, busy river-front harbour. But we won't be in the city for long. We're just waiting for a scientist called Dr Leon Portillo to come and take us to the research station, which is further upriver. And then we'll finally get to see the mysterious river dolphins!

The sound of voices from the deck made Jody look up. Was Dr Portillo here?

Quickly rolling off her bunk, Jody put her diary into the bag she'd already packed with the clothes and things she'd need for her time away. Resting beside it was Brittany's stuffed, much larger, carry-all.

Jody came into the main saloon just as her father came down the hatch. With him was a shortish, slim man with jet-black hair and olive skin.

'Everyone, this is Dr Leon Portillo,' said Craig. 'Dr Portillo, this is my wife, Dr Gina McGrath, and over there is the other scientist involved with "Dolphin Universe," Dr Jefferson Taylor . . .'

Dr Taylor hastily got up from the table and came over to shake hands with the newcomer. 'Very pleased to meet you, Dr Portillo,' he said, a polite smile stretching his round face.

'The pleasure is mine,' said the Venezuelan scientist. 'Please, call me Leon – all of you,' he urged. 'Otherwise there will be too many doctors on board!'

Craig quickly introduced everyone.

'Would you like a cup of coffee?' Gina offered. 'Or would you rather we got off straight away? I know it's a long journey to the research station – and we're all packed and ready to leave!'

'We sure are!' Sean declared enthusiastically.

Leon's smile faded. His eyes flickered uneasily around their eager faces. 'I'm afraid there's been a slight change of plan,' he said softly.

Jody's stomach clenched with anxiety. Surely the trip was still on?

'What's wrong?' Craig asked, frowning anxiously.

Leon turned to him. '*El Boto Grande* – that's the biggest of the boats at the research station – is down with engine trouble. So I've had to come to fetch you in *Tonina* instead – and she's much smaller,' Leon explained. He looked apologetic. 'So, I'm afraid that it won't be possible to transport eight people as we'd originally planned. Two of you will have to stay behind.'

2

'Well, I'm afraid *I* can't stay behind!' Dr Taylor blustered. 'As the representative of PetroCo – who are paying for this trip – I really must insist on being included in a visit to any research stations! Otherwise, they will think I'm not doing my job,' he added nervously.

'Yes, of course, Dr Taylor,' Craig said quickly. 'No one would dream of suggesting that you should stay behind!'

'I'll stay,' Maddie volunteered. 'I'm sure there's plenty to see and do around here, anyway.' She put her arm around Brittany and gave her a coaxing smile. 'What do you say we check out the sights of Ciudad Guyana together, girlfriend?'

Brittany's eyes widened. 'You think *I* should stay behind too?' She pulled away, shaking her head. '*I'm* not getting left behind!' she declared.

Jody's heart sank. It wasn't as if Brittany was even interested in dolphins. Why did she always have to make such a fuss! Jody looked anxiously at her mother.

Gina held up a hand and counted on her fingers. 'Me, Craig, Dr Taylor, Jody, Jimmy and Sean . . . that's six.' She looked at Brittany, then turned to Leon. 'The twins are double trouble, but they are quite small, if that would make a difference . . .'

'We're used to sharing,' Jimmy put in.

Leon smiled. Then, to everyone's relief, he nodded. 'OK – five and two half-passengers it is!'

'And that makes six!' Sean concluded triumphantly.

'I'll give you an A for your math today, Sean,' Maddie said, chuckling.

Jimmy's eyes widened as he thought of something. 'Hey, if you're not coming with us, Maddie, what about school?'

Maddie grinned. 'I'll let you into a secret,' she said. 'I wasn't going to give formal lessons during the trip anyway. You've all been working so hard lately, you've earned a break!'

Jimmy and Sean both cheered.

'But,' Maddie went on, shaking a warning finger at the boys, 'Just because I'm not along to give you lessons doesn't mean you stop learning! Keep your eyes and ears open while you're travelling, and find out all you can about life in this part of South America. This is your geography and natural history field trip.'

'I can't wait,' Jody said. 'There's going to be so much to put in my diary!'

Brittany rolled her eyes. 'Not for me! I'm just going to have fun!'

Within an hour they were all packed and settled on board *Tonina*. It could hardly have been more different from the ocean-going sailing yacht she was used to, Jody reflected. Leon's boat was a simple, wooden river launch, powered by an outboard motor. There were no cabins, just an open-sided canopy to provide shelter from sun and rain, with cushioned wooden benches for the passengers.

Brittany looked around doubtfully as Craig and Leon finished stowing bags away beneath the benches. 'Where will we sleep?' she asked.

'Don't worry – not on board,' Leon told her. 'We'll stop for the night.'

'Have a good time, love, and I'll see you back here next week,' said Harry. He wrapped his daughter in his arms for a big bear hug.

Brittany hugged him back. 'Bye, Daddy,' she said.

The engine gave a throaty roar. Harry leaped back to the dock where the rest of the crew of *Dolphin Dreamer* were waiting. Everyone – except Maddie, who was taking pictures – waved goodbye, and they were off!

Jody took a seat close to Leon. 'What does the name of the boat mean?' she asked.

'*Tonina* is one of the local names for the river dolphin,' Leon replied. 'The official, scientific name for the dolphin is *Inia geoffrensis*, but it is probably better known as the boto.' He shifted the throttle, his eyes on the river ahead, then continued. 'Botos live here in the Orinoco River, and in lots of tributaries and lakes as well. If you're lucky, you may see some today.'

Jody caught her breath with excitement. 'Do they like people?' she asked. 'Are they playful? Do they come right up to boats, like the dolphins in the ocean?'

'Jody, please, give the poor man a break!' Gina interrupted, laughing.

'Sorry,' Jody said, biting her lip. She felt embarrassed. 'I just love dolphins so much.'

'Me too,' Leon assured her, with a flashing smile. 'And there's nothing *I'd* rather talk about! But maybe we'd better wait for a quieter stretch of river . . .'

'OK,' Jody said. 'I'll let you concentrate on navigating!' She turned away to look out the side. She could see why Leon didn't want to be distracted: there was a lot of traffic on the river. Small speed boats zipped up and down, churning the brown water to froth. And there were many more open wooden boats like *Tonina* or a bit bigger, loaded down with passengers or with boxes of fruit, fish and vegetables.

If there were any botos in the area, Jody couldn't see them. The water looked filthy, not at all nice to swim in, with skims of shiny, rainbow-glinting oil on the surface, and plastic bottles and masses of soggy cardboard bobbing about.

Gradually they left the noisy, busy city behind. The background hum of people and industry died down. Buildings along the riverbanks became fewer. Instead of big factories belching smoke, and rows of warehouses, there were only a few isolated houses here and there. Even the river traffic began to fall away. Eventually, they were chugging along by themselves, past empty fields stretching away on either side of the dark brown river. The hot, humid air was still and quiet around them.

On the far bank, something splashed heavily in the water.

'What's that?' Sean asked.

'Looked like an alligator!' Jimmy cried, leaning out over the side to get a better look.

'Probably a caiman,' Leon replied.

'What's a caiman?' Sean asked.

'It's a type of crocodile,' Leon said. 'I'd guess that was a spectacled caiman you almost saw there . . . it's the most common of the caimans, and the closest in size to your North American alligator.'

Jimmy and Sean spot a Caiman!

'I wish I'd seen it,' Jimmy said wistfully. 'Reptiles are my favourites!'

Leon smiled. 'I'm sure you'll have another chance,' he said. 'There are lots of them in the river. You may even see some out of the river. People often catch them when they're small, and keep them as pets. They call them *babas*. My little sister used to have one.'

Jimmy and Sean stared at him open-mouthed. Then, as one, they turned towards their mother.

Quick as a flash, Gina said firmly, 'Don't even *think* about it!' Before the twins could try to argue with her, she said, 'So, Leon, did you grow up around here?'

'Not around here exactly,' he replied. 'My village was on the river, but hundreds of kilometres away, much further south, and deeper in the rainforest.'

'This doesn't look like rainforest,' Jimmy objected, waving his arm at the bare scrubland on the banks of the river. 'Where are all the trees?'

'They've been cut down,' Leon replied. 'Thousands of square kilometres of rainforest are destroyed every year.' He looked grim.

'Maddie told us about that, remember?' Brittany reminded the twins.

'But it looks so empty,' Jody said. She was puzzled. 'Did they clear it just for timber? Maddie said that the land is cleared for farming, or for pasture-land for cattle. But I don't see any people, or any crops, or any cows out there.'

'Maybe it's just being left to grow back?' Gina suggested, looking inquiringly at Leon.

He shook his head. 'Sadly, once the rainforest is cleared, it may never grow back,' he told them. 'And the land which is so rich in its natural state will only nourish crops for a few years. Within ten years, the soil is practically useless. And, of course, once the trees and other plants are gone, the animals disappear too.'

'But not the dolphins,' Jody said anxiously. 'Not the botos – they don't need the forest, do they?'

But Leon nodded. 'Everything in nature is interconnected,' he told her. 'The boto is different from other types of dolphin. It has adapted to life in the rainforest.'

'But they live in the *river*, not the forest,' Jody said, puzzled.

Leon smiled. 'During the rainy season, Jody, there's not such a big difference. A lot of the forest is flooded. Fish swim in among the trees – and the botos swim right after them!'

Jody's eyes widened. 'Really? The dolphins swim in the forest?' The idea was strange and magical. 'I wish I could see that!'

'You'll have to come back during the rainy season, then,' he told her. 'And maybe put on some scuba-diving gear!' He grinned. 'The botos aren't so easy to track when the rivers are high!'

'That's why it was recommended we come during the dry season,' Craig said. 'The river water-levels are falling, and that should give us our best chance to see some botos.'

'I can't *wait* to see them!' Jody said excitedly.

Leon smiled. 'Maybe this evening,' he said. 'I don't know where they hide during the heat of the day, but botos are most active early in the morning and then again at dusk. That's when we have most of our sightings.'

Hours passed as they chugged along the river. The day grew hotter and hotter, and they sweltered in the breezeless air.

Gradually Jody began to notice a change. The

barren scrubland alongside the river began to grow greener, lusher. Taller trees began to appear. As the air seemed to get thicker and wetter around them, they were gliding into uncut rainforest.

In spite of her discomfort, Jody felt her spirits rise. It was like another world here! She could hear loud shrieking cries coming from the trees – she wondered if they were birds or monkeys calling.

Suddenly, with a flash of blue and yellow, a brilliantly-coloured parrot swooped past, followed by four more. Everyone gasped.

'Wild parrots – in their natural habitat!' Dr Taylor exclaimed, and scrabbled in his briefcase for a pair of binoculars.

'Look at that big caiman!' Sean cried.

Leon was smiling broadly. 'Now I know I'm home,' he said. 'Welcome to the rainforest, my friends!'

3

Gina passed around sandwiches at lunchtime, although no one felt very hungry in the oppressive heat.

It was hard to made conversation when it was so hot, but Jody was determined to try. 'How did you first get interested in botos?' she asked Leon.

'I first met them when I was a small boy, out fishing with my father,' he replied. His dark eyes crinkled as he smiled, remembering. 'They were very playful. Often they would bump our canoe so hard I was sure they were trying to overturn us! But they never did, so I learned not to be frightened. Sometimes they would grab the end of the paddle and try to have a tug-of-war . . .' he laughed.

'Did you make friends with them?' Jody asked eagerly. Over the past few months she had made some unforgettable friends among the bottlenose and Atlantic spotted dolphins she had met. 'Are botos as friendly as other dolphins?'

'Botos are very different from marine dolphins,' Leon began. Then, noticing that Craig and Gina were listening to him as intently as Jody, he gave an apologetic little shrug. 'But I'm sure your parents know all about them! You don't want a lecture from me!'

'No, please, we'd love to hear more!' Craig said. He explained, 'My wife and I have always concentrated on the *delphinidae* throughout our career.' For the benefit of the twins and Brittany he added, '*Delphinidae* is the scientific name for the dolphins that live in the ocean. River dolphins have a different scientific classification, and we've never studied them.'

'And we've never seen a river dolphin,' Gina put in. 'We've read about them, and seen pictures, of course, but I think there's only one boto living in captivity in North America . . .'

'Botos don't do well in captivity,' Leon said firmly. 'Most die very quickly. And it's much better to study them in the wild!' He smiled. 'Well, I feel honoured to be your guide! How about you, Dr Taylor? Have you encountered river dolphins before?

Dr Taylor was scanning the shore through his binoculars, and did not respond.

Leon raised his voice to make sure it carried above the drone of the engine. 'Dr Taylor!'

Dr Taylor flinched in surprise, lowered his glasses, and turned to face the others. 'Oh, I'm sorry,' he said nervously. 'Were you speaking to me?'

'I was just wondering how much you knew about river dolphins.'

Looking rather embarrassed, Dr Taylor mumbled, 'Er, not really my specialty, you know . . .'

'That's fine,' Leon assured him. 'I was just about to launch into my "visitor guide to the pink dolphins" and I didn't want to bore anyone.'

'Did you say they were *pink*?' Jody asked. She was even *more* impatient to see one now!

Leon nodded. 'Their colour varies between pink and grey,' he said. 'Botos are born grey and gradually get pinker as they grow older. And botos in darker water, like this . . .' he gestured out at the muddy river, '. . . are pinker than botos who spend most of their time in clear water. That might be because in clear water, where they get more sun, they develop a sort of suntan.'

'Like people!' Brittany exclaimed.

Leon nodded. 'A boto also gets pinker when it is more active – and when it is excited – like a pale-skinned person blushing.' He grinned, and they all laughed – even Dr Taylor, who was mopping his own very pink face with a handkerchief.

'Cool!' said Sean.

'How else are they different from marine dolphins?' Jody asked.

'Well, because their environment is different, they need different tactics for food-finding,' Leon replied. 'What works well in the ocean wouldn't be so useful in a shallow lake or a flooded forest. Botos have very long, thin snouts, and they're very flexible. Unlike marine dolphins, a boto can turn its head one hundred and eighty degrees, from side to side. They can also paddle one flipper forward while paddling the other one backwards.'

'I'll bet that helps when they're chasing fish through the trees,' said Jimmy.

Leon grinned. 'Definitely,' he agreed. 'But botos aren't as speedy as marine dolphins,' he added. 'They swim much more slowly, don't dive as deeply, or jump as high out of the water. Mostly they just do a kind of bellyflop on the surface. Although,' he paused to grin at Jody, 'the young ones sometimes jump as much as a metre into the air. They're not particularly shy, and they seem curious enough about us to swim right up to boats and poke their heads up to get a look at us!'

Just then, Dr Taylor suddenly gave an excited yell.

'What's up?' asked Leon. 'Did you see one?'

Dr Taylor shouted in reply, 'There! Right there, by the shore!'

Jody caught her breath with excitement.

Everyone craned their necks to look where Dr Taylor was pointing.

But the water seemed undisturbed, as far as the eye could see.

'Oh, it's gone now,' said Dr Taylor. Sighing, he lowered his binoculars.

'Was it a boto?' Craig asked.

Dr Taylor looked startled. 'A what? Oh, the river dolphin – no, no, nothing like that.' He cleared his throat. 'I believe it was a Cocoi heron. Not exactly rare in these parts, I understand, but, still, the first time I'd seen one, so I became rather excited . . . Sorry about that!'

'That's OK,' said Gina, smiling. 'I didn't know you were a bird-watcher, Dr. Taylor.'

He nodded enthusiastically. 'It's a great hobby of mine. And this is a bird-watcher's paradise – why, did you know that there are more than a thousand different species of birds in the South American rainforest?'

'That's right,' said Leon. 'Only last month we had a couple of ornithologists from England staying at the research station.'

Dr Taylor's eyes sparkled with interest. 'Do you happen to remember . . . would you know . . . did they encounter any hoatzin?'

Leon nodded casually. 'Oh, yes, there's a little colony of hoatzin which nests not far from the station, on the edge of the lake. I've seen them myself.'

Dr Taylor clasped his pudgy hands beneath his

chin and gave a deep sigh. 'Oh, how exciting! Such a strange and unusual bird - quite prehistoric in many ways - I've always longed to see one - do you think I might have a chance . . .' his voice trailed off as he darted an anxious glance at Gina and Craig. 'Of course,' he added in a more business-like tone, 'I know we're really here to study dolphins, but . . .'

'I think we could probably fit a quick bird-watching expedition in between the dolphin-watches, just for you, Dr Taylor,' Leon said with a grin.

Dr Jefferson Taylor gave a happy sigh.

November 7 – afternoon – Orinoco River.
So far, Dr Taylor has spotted four or five different types of bird (he's keeping a list in a little notebook) but there's been no sign of a single boto!

It is incredibly *hot! Not a breath of wind. The canopy keeps the sun off, but there's nothing to break the heat. I'm dripping with sweat. I feel like I'm boiling – or poaching in my own juices. And it is still hours before the sun goes down. Even writing in this diary seems too much like hard work!*

The heat is making us all bad-tempered – except for

Leon, who doesn't seem to mind it. I guess he's used to it. Brittany is the worst – she's started to moan and groan and say she wishes she hadn't come after all . . .

If only a boto would come along and cheer us all up!

'Here, Jody, have something to drink.'

Jody put down her diary and gratefully accepted the bottle of juice her mother offered.

'No thanks,' Brittany said when Gina offered her the same.

'I really think you should,' Gina said firmly. 'It's important not to get dehydrated.'

Brittany shrugged and took the drink. 'How long till we get there?' she wanted to know.

'Not until tomorrow evening,' Leon replied.

Brittany made a face. 'I mean where we're staying tonight; how long till we get there?'

'We'll stop before sundown,' he told her. 'Two or three hours from now.'

She sighed heavily. 'I sure wish this boat was air-conditioned!'

'Let's not dwell on the heat,' Gina said. 'We need something to take our minds off it.'

'I could tell you some stories about the boto,' Leon offered.

Brittany groaned. 'Oh, dolphins! Haven't we heard enough about them?'

'*Brittany*,' Gina said in a warning voice.

Brittany hunched her shoulders and looked mutinous, but said nothing more.

'The stories I had in mind are a little different,' Leon said calmly. 'I was thinking of the stories of my people – legends that are full of magic and romance.'

'That sounds great,' Craig said enthusiastically.

Jody nodded eagerly. Even Brittany looked interested. Only Dr Taylor looked sceptical, but for once he didn't object, as he usually did, to something 'unscientific'.

Leon began: 'This is the story of my grandfather, who swore it really happened. And everyone in the village believed him, because my grandfather was a very wise and powerful man. He was a Piaroa Indian, and the shaman of his tribe.'

'What's a shaman?' asked Sean with a puzzled frown.

'A man with special, spiritual powers,' Leon

explained. 'A healer. They have to study hard – but not at a university, like I did. My grandfather spent many days alone in the jungle, learning from the plants and animals. But he always said that his special powers were a gift from the boto who had befriended him.'

Jody caught her breath with surprise.

'You see, my people believe that the boto is a magical creature,' Leon went on. 'They say that the boto can change his shape, and walk on the land in the form of a man – or a woman.' He paused to drink from a bottle of water.

Then he went on. 'When he was a very young man, hardly more than a boy, my grandfather saved the life of an injured dolphin. About a week later, one evening, when he was walking beside the river, he met a beautiful girl dressed all in white. She had pale, pinkish skin, fair hair, and blue eyes.' He looked at Brittany. 'Rather like you, I would imagine.'

Brittany flushed at his attention.

'But remember,' Leon continued, 'this was before the *civilizados* came to my grandfather's village, and he had never seen anyone who wasn't dark-skinned like himself. He knew the botos were magical, so he was not surprised when she revealed that she was the dolphin whose life he had saved – she even showed him the scar on her arm! She wanted to thank him for saving her, and invited him to visit her home at the bottom of the river. So, he went with her.'

Leon paused again. Everyone in the boat was silent, leaning towards him, hanging on his words. He smiled slightly and continued the story.

'Under the water was the most amazing, magical city. Life was very easy there. No one had to work hard. It was a wonderful place. My grandfather learned many secret things. He said he could have stayed there forever, as the beautiful dolphin-girl loved him, but he decided to return home and use his new knowledge to help his people. And so he did. But throughout the rest of his life, he would sometimes be visited by a strange, fair woman, dressed all in white . . .'

Jody looked at Brittany, sitting there in white shirt, shorts, socks and trainers. What a spooky coincidence that she'd chosen to dress all in white today.

In fact, everyone in the boat was looking at

Brittany as Leon finished his story.

She flushed even more, and turned abruptly, leaning out over the side as if in search of a cooling breeze.

At that moment there was a splashing sound. Suddenly three small, greyish dolphins appeared, leaping high in the air, twisting and turning as if putting on a show before splashing heavily down into the water again.

Brittany yelped as a spray of water cascaded over her. Then, unexpectedly, she laughed. 'Hey, that feels good! Thanks for cooling me off, guys!'

Jody laughed, too. She was pleased that Brittany was being a good sport for once, and she felt excited by this first, unexpected sighting. But something was puzzling her. As the dolphins swam rapidly away, she turned to Leon to ask, 'Were those botos? I thought . . .'

Leon shook his head firmly. 'No, those were some of the other dolphins we get in the river. They're called "Tucuxi" and they're not true river dolphins – not like the boto, which has evolved to live only in rivers. Tucuxi are found along the coast, as well, and they are relatives of the marine dolphins. You might have noticed that they look rather like a small bottlenose dolphin.'

'I wish I'd managed to get a picture,' Gina said ruefully, holding the camera she'd just pulled out of her bag. 'But they were too quick for me!'

'There will be other chances,' Leon told her. 'We often spot them feeding in small groups alongside the botos.

'It's the botos that are hardest to photograph,' he went on. 'They're not shy, but they don't spend much time above the surface. You have to get your camera ready to shoot at the very first sight of them!' He broke off, his attention caught by something else. 'Brittany, that's not a good idea!' he said sharply.

Brittany had been leaning over the edge of the boat. She straightened up now and gave him a puzzled look. 'I was only splashing a little water on my face,' she said. 'To cool down. The dolphins gave me the idea. Don't worry, I'm not going to drink it!' She leaned back over the side, trailing one hand in the water.

'It's dangerous,' Leon replied. 'You don't want the piranha to bite off your fingers, do you?'

Brittany laughed, and continued to trail her hand

Brittany tests the water...

through the water. 'Oh, sure!'

'I'm serious,' he said. 'These waters are full of biting fish.'

'Yeah, and there's an underwater city with dolphin-people who look just like me,' she replied in a bantering tone.

Leon frowned slightly and turned to Gina. 'Maybe if you tell her–'

But it was too late. Brittany gave a blood-curdling scream.

4

Brittany yanked her hand out of the water, still screaming.

With a sickening lurch of her stomach, Jody saw the bright red blood dripping from Brittany's hand.

'There's a first-aid kit just under your seat,' Leon told Craig.

Gina moved quickly to take charge of Brittany. 'Let me see, sweetie - and please stop screaming, that doesn't help,' she added, gently but firmly.

Brittany gulped, and burst into noisy sobs.

'It's only a little cut - you haven't lost a finger,'

Gina reassured her. 'In fact, you won't even need stitches, thank goodness! Craig, could you pass me a bandage? And some antiseptic?'

They all watched, wide-eyed and silent, as Gina dealt swiftly and efficiently with Brittany's wound. In a few moments the injured finger was neatly bound in gauze and tape.

Brittany had stopped crying, but now she was shivering. 'I feel awful,' she moaned. 'Maybe I caught something – rabies or some other horrible disease . . .'

'It's the shock, honey,' Gina told her. She put an arm around Brittany and hugged her, then looked over at Jody. 'Sweetheart, could you find a soft drink for Brittany?'

Jody nodded and made her way to the cool-box, where she found a bottle of Coke.

'Did she really get bitten by a piranha?' Jimmy asked Leon in an awed voice.

'Maybe,' Leon told him. 'But there are other fish with teeth which aren't flesh-eaters. Mostly they feed on fruit, seeds and berries which fall into the water. One of them might have mistaken Brittany's finger for something good to eat.'

'Oh, I hate this place!' Brittany moaned. 'I wish I'd never come!'

'Please don't judge it so quickly,' said Leon. 'You've had a bad experience. It is true there are dangers here - but there are also many wonders in the river - wait and see!'

Brittany huddled against Gina for comfort. She looked unconvinced.

November 7 – continued.
Well, so much for my dream of swimming with the botos! The thought of all those biting fish makes my skin crawl. It's too dangerous to go into the water, so we'll have to do all our dolphin-watching from the boat. If they ever show themselves, that is!

I asked Leon if piranhas were a danger to the botos. He said botos usually eat piranhas (along with about 50 other species of fish!). But if a boto is wounded, it could be in trouble. The blood will attract piranhas which will swim up in a big group and start nibbling. If the dolphin is too weak to escape, they can eat him alive! Yuck!

Jody looked up from her diary when she heard Leon say, 'We'll stop here for the night.' He switched off the engine. A moment later, with a soft jolting movement, the boat ran aground.

Leon leaped over the side and reached out to help Gina come ashore.

'Where are we staying?' Brittany asked as she followed Gina out of the boat.

Jody was wondering the same thing. She could see nothing but forest as she gazed around. There was no sign of any building, or even a road that might lead to one.

'Here,' Leon replied, with a gesture at the trees. 'We'll put up the hammocks.'

Sean and Jimmy gave excited cheers. 'Oh, boy, we get to camp out!'

Jody thought it sounded like fun, too. She glanced at Brittany, meaning to trade a smile, but saw that the other girl had gone very still.

Dr Taylor also looked unhappy. 'Dear me, I'm not very good at roughing it!' he exclaimed nervously. 'Nobody warned me . . .'

'There's no other option, I'm afraid,' Leon said, looking apologetic. 'The research station is still a day's journey away, and the nearest village is nearly that far. Luckily, we should have a dry night. And hammocks are much better for sleeping than the hard seats on the boat!'

'Absolutely,' Craig said firmly. 'We're going to have a great time. Now, we'd better get our camp set up before dark – Leon, tell us what you want us to do!'

'First thing is to fetch everything out of the boat, and put up the hammocks,' Leon said, leading the way.

Jody was eager to help, but she hung back. Brittany looked pale and frightened. And it wasn't like her to be so quiet. When she was unhappy about something, she usually made sure everyone knew it!

'What's wrong?' Jody asked quietly.

Brittany turned unhappy blue eyes on her. 'Aren't you scared to spend the night in this jungle?'

Jody shook her head. 'No. Leon's done it loads of times. He'll tell us if there's anything dangerous . . . we'll just have to do what he says.'

'But he doesn't even have a gun,' Brittany protested. 'What if we get attacked by a jaguar!'

Craig, coming past with an armload of supplies, overheard this. He stopped. 'We'd have to be pretty lucky to spot a jaguar,' he said with a friendly grin.

'Lucky!' Brittany stared at him in disbelief. 'They're killers!'

Craig shook his head. 'Jaguars don't attack people,' he said. 'In fact, they keep well out of our way. Too many of them have been killed for their fur. People are a much greater danger to them than they are to us – and I think they know it!'

'Well, OK,' said Brittany with a grudging nod. 'But what about snakes?'

'We have poisonous snakes in Florida,' Craig reminded her. 'Given half a chance, most snakes will keep out of your way. They're not usually aggressive. Just be sensible, same as you would if you were camping out at home.' With that, he walked on.

Brittany, gazing after him, didn't look completely convinced. But she didn't look so frightened now, either, Jody thought. 'Have you ever been camping before?' she asked curiously.

Brittany nodded. 'A couple of times, with Daddy. Once he took me to the Everglades.' She paused. 'It was fun,' she admitted, seeming surprised by the memory. Then she looked wistful. 'I wish my dad was here now!'

Jody patted her shoulder. 'Yeah, but you'll have

some great stories to tell him when we get back! Come on, let's go help set up camp!'

'Now we have to catch our dinner,' Jimmy announced as Craig and Leon finished building a small cooking fire down on the sandbank.

'Oh, there's no need for that,' Gina said. 'We've brought plenty of food with us.'

The twins looked disappointed. 'But we wanted to fish!' Sean exclaimed.

'Why not?' said Leon. 'I can tell you which ones are good to eat.' He glanced around. 'Anyone else want to come?'

'I'll stay and tend the fire,' Gina offered. She gave Craig a teasing punch on the arm. 'Go on, I know you're dying to go fishing!'

'She knows me too well,' laughed Craig. 'I'd love to try my luck on the Orinoco! How about you, Jody?'

At home, Jody sometimes went fishing with her father and brothers, but she shook her head. 'I'd rather watch for dolphins.' She glanced at Leon. 'You said they're most active at dusk?'

He nodded. 'How about you, Brittany?'

The other girl quickly shook her head. 'No thanks. I'll stay with Aunt Gina.'

'Dr Taylor?' Leon turned to him.

The portly scientist shook his head. 'I've never seen the appeal of fishing . . . I'd rather find a quiet spot and watch for birds.'

'OK,' said Leon. 'Keep that fire burning - with any luck, we'll be back with some treats very soon!'

Gina grinned. 'I'll keep my trusty can-opener handy, just in case you don't!'

As her dad and brothers trooped off with Leon, Jody dug out her diary and pen from her bag and set off in the opposite direction along the bank of the river.

'Don't go far,' Gina said warningly. 'It'll be dark soon, and it would be very easy to get lost!'

'Don't worry,' Jody replied. 'I'll follow the river. Give me a whistle when you want me back.'

Jody walked through the rainforest, being careful to keep the river in view on her right-hand side. It was slow going. Vines, creepers, tree-roots and bushes all grew together in a lush tangle. She had to be careful where she put her feet. After a few minutes she was relieved to spot a fallen tree. It made a natural bench for her to perch on, and gave her a good, clear view of the river. She settled down to watch.

Without the constant droning noise of the boat's engine, the gentler sounds of the river and the rainforest could finally be heard. There was the sound of the water lapping at the shore, bird-calls from the trees behind her, and a steady chirping which she thought might be tree-frogs.

A rustle in the leaves at her feet made her look down. Jody glimpsed a brilliant green head with two bright golden eyes. She caught her breath. It was some sort of large lizard. With a swish of its tail, it darted forward and vanished into the undergrowth.

A loud, eerie cry made her look up. But she couldn't see anything moving in the dark green canopy of leaves. Another eerie cry came from the forest behind. Heart pounding, Jody twisted her head around, but again she could see nothing.

All of a sudden, she felt nervous. She was very aware of being alone. Daylight was rapidly fading. The sun had vanished behind the trees, and the sky above the dark river had taken on a rosy glow. Maybe it was time to head back.

Then she heard a new sound: a soft, gentle sigh, which seemed to come from the river.

She heard it again, and, as she leaned forward, peering intently, she saw the water ripple. Something broke through to the surface. It was large and sleek, a gently curved shape which was the same rosy pink colour as the evening sky. A boto?

With a whooshing sound, it slipped back beneath the water and vanished.

Jody waited, holding her breath, staring until she thought her eyes would drop out, but the dolphin – if that's what it had been – did not appear again.

'Yes, it probably was a boto,' Leon told her when she later described what she had seen. 'I often hear them but don't see them. It's no wonder they have such a magical reputation, the way they appear and disappear so suddenly!'

When Jody had arrived back at camp, the twins were proudly showing off their catch: six fish, and only two of them the same kind! Leon had caught another four, and Craig had two, the biggest of the lot.

'That's amazing!' Gina exclaimed. 'You were gone

A boto makes a rare appearance!

barely half an hour – I've known you boys to go out fishing all day and come back with nothing!'

'That's the Orinoco for you,' said Leon, smiling. 'And at this time of year, with the river low, the fish are especially hungry. That makes them easy to catch, since they'll bite anything that looks at all good to eat.'

'Like a finger,' Jimmy said. He pointed out one of the largest fish. 'Look at the teeth on that one, Brittany! It might be the same kind that bit you!'

'Now you can have your revenge by eating it,' Leon said with a teasing smile, as he and Craig gutted and cleaned the fish ready for cooking.

Brittany shuddered. 'No thanks!'

Darkness fell swiftly. They all gathered more closely around the campfire as the fish cooked.

Leon told them about the work of the research station, which he'd helped to establish three years earlier. 'You know, it's surprising how little is still known about the boto,' he said.

'Are they an endangered species, like the river dolphins in other parts of the world?' Gina asked.

Jody was relieved to see Leon shake his head. But her heart sank when he added, 'Not officially listed as endangered, but their numbers are low, and it's probably only a matter of time . . .' He went on to explain: 'The botos' habitat is changing. Forest is being cut down to create more land for farming; dams are being built to provide hydro-electric power. Many fish species are dying out, sometimes because of over-fishing.' Leon sighed. 'The botos will find it harder to live. Already, they are in competition with the local fishermen – or at least, that's how the fishermen see it! The dolphins have learned to steal fish from nets, and in doing so, sometimes tear them. Of course, the nets cost money, and many fishermen can barely make a living as it is, so they are furious at the botos for destroying their nets, and may try to kill them.'

'But the botos don't tear the net deliberately, do they?' asked Jody.

'No, they're simply trying to reach the fish,' Leon agreed. 'But there's another problem with the nets: usually dolphins are very good at detecting dangers underwater, and staying out of the way. But sometimes fishermen will set their nets in such a way that the dolphins can't detect them so well . . . or set them in a narrow, shallow channel, so that in the dry season, especially, the boto can't avoid it – they're trapped before they know it.'

'What happens then?' Jody asked anxiously.

'Well, sometimes they manage to escape, ripping the net with their teeth to get out. At other times . . . they can't get loose, and if they're trapped below the water, they drown,' Leon replied.

Jody caught her breath.

'But things may be getting better,' Leon went on. 'At least around here. Since we set up the research centre we've been working with the local people, talking to them about ways of catching fish without endangering the dolphins.'

'It sounds like you're doing good work,' said Gina.

'We're trying,' Leon replied. 'I'm sure there's a way for people and dolphins to live together in harmony – but it will only happen if the people who live here agree it is important.'

'What do you think – are these fish about done?' asked Craig, prodding one with a long fork.

The smell rising from the grilling fish was delicious. Jody felt her mouth watering.

'I think so,' said Leon, smiling. 'Let's dig in.'

* * *

Jody woke to a faint crawling sensation on her skin.

When she opened her eyes, it was too dark to see anything. She felt disorientated. Where was she? This wasn't her bunk on board *Dolphin Dreamer*.

Then, in a rush, it all came back to her. She was in a hammock, camping out in the rainforest, on the bank of the Orinoco River.

And the crawling sensation was . . . ANTS!

With a yell, Jody sat bolt upright, causing her hammock to rock wildly. She began brushing at her arms and legs, sending the ants flying.

'Hey, what's the matter?' Craig's voice, sleepy and alarmed, sounded close at hand. He was in the hammock next to Jody's. Then he, too, gave a yell.

A light flared. Gina sat up in her hammock, on the other side of Craig's, holding a torch. Her black hair was a tangled cloud around her startled face. 'What's going on?' she demanded.

'Ants!' Craig shouted. 'They're everywhere!'

Another torch shone: it was Leon, on the ground and fully dressed, even wearing his boots. He came closer, directing the light at Craig. 'Oh, they're only the little ones,' he said calmly. 'They won't hurt you.'

'I'm not going to give them the chance!'

Craig declared, slapping at himself.

'Shine the light over here,' Jody begged. 'I can't see!'

On her other side, Brittany sat up. 'What's wrong?' she asked sleepily.

'Ants,' Jody informed her. She shuddered. Although she couldn't see any more of them, she seemed to feel them running all over her still. 'Would you look at my back and see if there are any there?' she asked Brittany.

'I don't want them to get on me!' Brittany objected, shrinking back.

'I'll do it,' Sean said. He swung out of the hammock he'd shared with his brother and hurried over to Jody's, his own miniature torch at the ready.

After a brief inspection he announced, 'Nope, I can't see any. There's loads crawling up this tree, though, right above your head!'

Jody shuddered again. She wished she could have a shower, so she could be sure the ants really were all gone. However, as the only place to bathe was a river teeming with biting fish, she'd just have to put up with the lingering itching sensation.

Craig sighed. 'So Jody and I had the bad luck

to sling our hammocks on the local ant superhighway . . . Well, I guess we'd better move them . . .'

'There's no point,' said Leon. 'Since we're all awake, I suggest we pack up and get back on the river as soon as possible.'

'But it's the middle of the night!' Gina objected.

Leon grinned. 'It's four o'clock in the morning,' he corrected her. 'The day starts early in the tropics – it's a good idea to miss the worst heat of the day,' he explained.

'Dr Taylor isn't awake yet,' Jimmy announced. 'Want me to wake him up?'

'No, honey!' Gina said quickly. 'Your dad will do that.'

Craig rolled his eyes. 'Thanks a lot!'

'You're welcome, darling,' she smiled sweetly.

Soon they were back on the river again. Jody was glad; she felt far too wide-awake now to go back to sleep! Only Dr Taylor kept yawning and grumbling about the lack of coffee.

Jody noticed her mother was checking her camera by one of the dim lights on board. 'Isn't it kind of dark to be taking pictures?' she asked curiously.

Gina smiled at her. 'I want to be ready as soon as the sun comes up, in case we glimpse some of these mysterious botos!'

Sean and Jimmy, both excited to be on a night-time river cruise, were shining their torches out into the darkness. Suddenly one of the boys gave a yell.

'What is it, son?' asked Craig.

'Spooky eyes! Look!' Jimmy replied, directing the beam onto the dark water.

'Millions of 'em,' added Sean.

Jody caught her breath. Not millions, as her brother said, but at least a dozen pair of amber eyes glowed unblinkingly from the water's edge. She shivered. They *were* spooky! 'What are they?' she asked.

'Caimans,' Leon told them.

'Really big ones, too,' said Sean. 'I bet they'd try to eat us if we fell in the water!'

'They might,' Leon agreed. 'They're certainly not the kind you should try to play with!'

Before long. *Tonina* moved into deeper water, and out of the range of the evil-looking eyes.

Jody felt herself growing sleepy, lulled by the

steady movement of the boat. No one spoke. Even the twins were quiet. Brittany, slumped beside her, seemed to have nodded off. Then, a loud, donkey-like braying sound echoed across the water, startling them all wide awake.

'What was *that*?' Gina gasped.

'Sounded like a donkey in trouble,' Craig said.

'That, unless I'm very much mistaken, was a horned screamer,' said Dr Taylor, sounding excited. He fumbled in his bag for his binoculars. 'It's an enormous bird, usually seen perched on top of bushes or trees along the waterside. Oh, I would love to spot one! Luckily there is some light . . .'

As he spoke, Jody realised that the darkness wasn't as deep as before. A thin, grey light revealed the dark outlines of trees and bushes along the shore, and it was getting lighter by the minute.

It was hard to be sure above the drone of the engine, but Jody thought she heard a gentle, soft sighing sound nearby. She leaned over the side of the boat and saw the water ripple as something slipped beneath the surface. 'I think I saw a boto,' she said urgently, trying to follow the movement in the water.

Gina moved to her side, camera at the ready. 'Where?' she asked.

Jody pointed. 'It was there – but it's gone now. Maybe it will come up again.'

Suddenly the engine cut out. Silence descended. The boat rocked gently.

'What's wrong?' Dr Taylor asked in alarm.

'Nothing at all,' Leon told him in a reassuring voice. 'I've just stopped to give Gina a chance to get some pictures when the botos come up for air. Dawn and dusk are the times of day when the botos are most active. Maybe they'll pop up to take a look at us. We'd miss them if we kept going.'

Jody thought of her days at sea, and how much fun the bottlenose and Atlantic spotted dolphins had seemed to have racing *Dolphin Dreamer*. 'Don't the botos like to swim alongside moving boats?' she asked Leon.

He shook his head. 'Botos aren't speedy creatures like the dolphins you are used to,' he explained. 'They generally swim at a rate of only two to three kilometres an hour. They couldn't keep up with a motorboat, not even a fairly slow one like this.'

'There's one!' Gina gasped. Then she sighed,

lowering her camera. 'Gone again!'

'I saw something – I think it was a tail,' Jimmy announced.

'There!' exclaimed Dr Taylor. They all looked at him and saw that he had his binoculars trained on the shore. 'My first green ibis!' he announced triumphantly.

'That's nice, Dr Taylor,' said Craig tactfully. 'But it would be helpful if we could all concentrate on the water, instead of the air or the shore. After all, we're here to study the botos – not birds.'

The portly scientist looked embarrassed. 'Yes, yes, of course. I'm so sorry . . . I'll concentrate my attention on the water, from now on!' He began to fiddle with the settings on his binoculars.

Jody heard the now-familiar sighing sound from the water right beside her. She turned to look.

The dark water rippled. Then a pink, rounded head with a long, thin snout appeared, rising smoothly straight up out of the water. Jody held her breath with excitement. The pink dolphin looked directly at her with bright, intelligent eyes. It was so close that if she put out her hand she could touch it.

Jody heard the click of her mother's camera.

Then, as swiftly and quietly as it had appeared, the boto dropped down in the water again, vanishing without even a splash.

'Wow, I'm glad I got that one on film!' Gina exclaimed. She turned to Leon. 'It was spyhopping! Oceanic dolphins do it all the time, but I didn't think spyhopping was boto behaviour.'

'Oh, they rise up like that when there's something on the surface they want to get a good look at,' Leon told her, smiling broadly. 'I got the feeling he was as curious about you as you are about him! He may have recognised the boat and wondered who was on board today!'

With a whoosh of breath, the dolphin surged up again. This time they saw only the curve of his back with its low dorsal ridge, before he vanished, leaving behind a spray of fine mist.

'There's one on this side!' Dr Taylor called excitedly.

Jody caught only a glimpse of a flipper before it was gone again.

For the next ten minutes as the sun rose higher, the botos played 'catch me if you can' around the boat, swimming back and forth beneath the dark brown river, surfacing for a few seconds with a sighing breath of air before disappearing again.

'Oh, this is maddening!' Gina groaned. 'The light is perfect, the botos are here, but – they're such teases! I can't even tell how many there are! You'd think they didn't want their pictures taken!' she joked.

'Shall we move on, then?' Leon suggested. 'We still have a long way to go.'

'I think so,' said Craig.

As Gina nodded her agreement, Leon started up the engine.

Jody leaned over the side, gazing wistfully after the elusive botos.

November 8 – late morning – Orinoco River.
Boto (Inia geoffrensis)
Botos are so gorgeous! But they're so hard to get a good look at, that it's no wonder some people think they are magical, shape-changing animals! I'm really looking forward to getting to the research station – Leon says we'll be there by late afternoon, so there should be enough time before dark to go out and watch the botos who live nearby. We haven't seen any more botos on

our journey today. I guess they're keeping cool, out of the heat of the day. It's getting hotter by the minute.

Jody leaned over the side of the boat, trying to make the most of the little breeze.

'We're almost home,' Leon announced. 'We should be at the research station in half an hour or so.'

'Thank goodness,' Brittany muttered. 'I thought we'd never get off this boat!'

'Yes, we're all looking forward to it,' Gina said quickly. 'How many people are based at the station?'

'Two other researchers, besides me,' Leon replied. 'Others come and go throughout the year, but at the moment there's no one else. So there's plenty of space for you all.'

'And more than one shower, I hope?' Craig mopped his brow with a handkerchief as he spoke.

Leon laughed. 'En suite bathrooms come as standard in our luxurious residence,' he said, making them all laugh.

'Hey, look, there's somebody waving at us on the shore,' Jimmy announced. 'Over there, look!'

Jody followed her little brother's pointing finger.

She saw a boy of about her own age waving his arms wildly and shouting.

Leon shaded his eyes against the sun. 'Why, that looks like Juan! He's a local boy who often comes round to help out at the station.'

'I don't think he's just waving,' Gina said, frowning. 'He seems upset.'

Leon turned the boat and headed it towards the riverbank. As they came closer, they could hear the boy was shouting, '*Ayudame, por favor!*'

Spanish wasn't Jody's greatest subject, but even she understood what that meant.

The boy was shouting, 'Help me, please!'

5

Leon ran the boat ashore on a sandbank. He switched off the motor and leaped out. 'Stay here, please,' he said. 'I'll see what the problem is.'

Juan rushed forward and spoke urgently to Leon in Spanish.

Jody couldn't understand a word of it. She looked at Brittany, who was listening with her head cocked. 'Do you know what he's saying?' she asked.

Brittany nodded. 'I think so,' she said. 'It's about a boto. He says it's in big trouble . . .'

Leon came striding back to the boat and spoke to Craig urgently. 'Please, could you look after the boat for me? Juan has found a dolphin trapped in a fishing net – I'm going to try to free it.'

'Do you need some help?' Gina asked.

Leon nodded. 'Yes, it could be useful to have someone else to help hold the animal still while I cut the net.'

'I'll come with you, then,' Gina said, clambering out of the boat.

'Can we come too?' asked Jimmy.

'No,' Craig said firmly. 'You guys stay right here with me. I don't want you getting in Leon's way.'

Jody was also halfway over the side of the boat as he said that. She hesitated, and looked anxiously at her father. She was desperate to help. She couldn't bear to wait behind when there was a dolphin that needed help! Craig caught her eye and nodded his head slightly.

Smiling her thanks, Jody jumped down and ran after her mother and Leon.

Jody was puzzled because they seemed to be moving away from the river. However, after a few moments she saw that they were heading towards a sort of shallow canal which curved round to meet the river slightly further down.

'Juan found the boto about half an hour ago, tangled in a fishing net,' Leon explained. 'He's been trying to untangle it, but couldn't do it. He doesn't have a knife or anything to cut through the net. He was just heading back to his village to get help when he spotted us.'

'Will the boto be all right?' Jody asked anxiously.

'Fortunately the water is shallow so it is able to breathe,' Leon told her. 'But we have no idea how long it has been caught, or if it is badly injured.' he concluded grimly.

Jody's heart hammered in her chest.

'Let's hope we're not too late,' said Gina quietly.

Up ahead, Juan was beckoning to them. They hurried to join him.

He was standing in the channel, where the water came barely to his waist, and his arms were around the long, greyish-pink body of a boto. It lay still, without struggling, as if it knew the boy wanted to help. Jody could see its blowhole opening and closing like a tiny mouth as it breathed.

'Why, it's Ocho!' Leon exclaimed, recognising the dolphin. To Gina and Jody he explained, 'I've known this one since he was born. He's still very young –

just over a year old.' He slipped down into the water beside Juan and stroked the trapped boto, running a keen eye over his body. In a gentle voice he murmured, 'You should have stayed close to your mama, not come so far chasing fishes!'

'What do you want us to do?' Jody asked.

'Get ready to help Juan gently hold Ocho still, in case he starts to struggle while I'm cutting the net,' Leon replied. 'He seems calm now, but he could be just exhausted. You never know. Be very calm yourself, and try not to add to his stress.'

Jody got into the water beside Juan. She moved slowly, carefully, keeping an anxious eye on Ocho. She wondered how long the boto had been trapped before Juan found him. Lying in such shallow water meant he was able to breathe, but it also meant he'd been exposed to the sun and the full heat of the day – and she knew that could be dangerous.

As Leon got out his knife, Juan looked anxious. He spoke urgently in Spanish. Leon replied briefly, and bent over the net. Taking great care to avoid damaging the dolphin's tender skin, he made a few cuts in the netting. Within seconds, the net fell away from the dolphin's sides. Ocho was free.

But the dolphin remained unmoving in the shallow, muddy water.

Jody chewed her lip anxiously as she waited for Ocho to swim away. Was he injured? Had they arrived too late?

She moved back, in case the dolphin was afraid of her, noticing that her mother and Juan were doing the same.

Suddenly, Ocho gave a wheezing snort and rolled onto his side. His powerful flippers – so much bigger than the ones on the dolphins she'd been used to – flexed. He pushed himself away from the shore. Then he gave an awkward-looking leap that ended with a belly-flop, and splashed them all with water.

Jody barely flinched; she was concentrating too hard on what the boto would do next. Was he injured at all? With a powerful flex of his tail, Ocho shot away down the narrow, shallow channel, heading for the river. She gave a deep sigh of relief. She really felt like cheering!

'Back to find his mama now, I hope,' said Leon, smiling. 'We'll look for him tomorrow morning, and make sure he's not suffering any bad effects.' Reaching to give Gina a hand in climbing out of the channel, he added, 'Juan, would you like a lift with us to the research station?' He repeated his offer to the boy in Spanish.

Juan nodded. '*Si, si, con muchas gracias*,' he accepted politely. But he was staring worriedly at the slashed net. He said something else to Leon in Spanish, and the man replied.

'What are they talking about?' Jody asked her mother in a whisper.

'Juan says the man who owns the slashed net can't afford to buy a new one,' Gina explained as she listened to the conversation.

Jody frowned. 'Well, he shouldn't have set it where a dolphin could get trapped in it,' she said hotly. 'It serves him right!'

Gina shook her head, although she looked sympathetic. 'Life isn't that simple, sweetheart. The local people need to fish to survive – just as much as the dolphins do! But I think it will be all right this time,' she added, pausing to listen to Leon's reply to Juan.

Jody saw that Juan looked very relieved, and was nodding eagerly. 'What did Leon say?' she asked.

'I think somebody needs to work a little harder on her Spanish,' Gina said teasingly. Then she relented and translated. 'Leon says that his organisation will pay for a new net – this time. But he says Juan must remind the local fishermen not to set their nets in these narrow channels where it is too hard for the dolphins to avoid them in the dry season,' Gina explained. 'He says, tell them to remember the discussions they've had about safer ways of using nets,' she finished.

That settled, they all walked back down to the river and rejoined the others on board *Tonina*.

Leon pushed the boat back into the river, jumped aboard, and started up the engine. Then he introduced Juan to everyone. 'I first met Juan a couple of years ago, during a visit to his school,' he explained. 'Part of our work at the research station is to help local people figure out the best ways of preserving the environment. So we make regular visits to the village school. Juan was absolutely fascinated by botos even before we came, but once he learned about our research – well, there was no stopping him!' Leon grinned and looked to Juan for agreement.

But Juan didn't notice. He was staring, awestruck, at Brittany.

Jody realised he had not taken his eyes off her since he'd arrived. She couldn't tell if Brittany was aware of his interest or not. She wore a faintly bored expression on her face as she gazed out at the passing scenery. She could have been miles away, or only pretending not to notice.

When Juan did not respond to Leon, Craig jumped in to fill the pause. 'So, does Juan spend all his time rescuing dolphins in need?' he asked with a friendly grin.

'He spends most of his spare time helping us at the research station,' Leon replied. 'Isn't that right, Juan?'

Juan did not reply. He was edging along the bench, inching closer to Brittany. Very slowly, as if approaching a timid animal, he stretched out one hand to touch her long, fair hair.

Brittany flinched and pulled back, glaring at him.

Juan looked sorry. '*Lo siento mucho!*' He murmured in apology. '*Por favor* . . .'

Jody expected Brittany to tell him off in no uncertain terms. But the girl hesitated. And when

Juan gets friendly with Britt

she spoke, her voice was unexpectedly gentle. The other surprise was that she spoke in Spanish.

Juan gasped, his eyes widening in astonishment that this stranger spoke his own language! He responded with a torrent of rapid Spanish.

Brittany giggled. She shook her head. Then, in her slow, careful Spanish she begged him to slow down. She explained that she had been studying Spanish for only a year.

'Then I'll speak in English,' Juan announced.

'Because I have been studying your language for two whole years, ever since meeting Leon and Carlos and Julie. Most of the people who come to the research station speak English. Carlos - he comes from Caracas - he says English is the international language of business and science. I want to be a scientist, so I should know English - you understand?' He gazed at her, dazzled. 'But I am very surprised that you speak Spanish! That is amazing!'

Brittany shrugged. 'They made us study it at my school, that's all.' She looked away from his adoring gaze, obviously uncomfortable. 'Hey, Leon,' she called. 'How much farther do we have to go?'

'Not long now,' he promised.

Within a few minutes they arrived at an intersection with another river. Jody glimpsed a flash of pink and grey. Moments later, there was the sight of a broad, powerful flipper as another boto rolled in the water. Another one popped up, its long-snouted face seeming to give them a cheeky grin before disappearing again. Everywhere they looked there were splashings and snortings, and brief, magical glimpses of the big, long-snouted pink and grey creatures.

'The botos often gather where two rivers intersect,' Leon explained, as Gina grabbed her camera and began snapping away. 'It's a good place for them to fish.

'So, of course,' he added, 'it also makes a good place for a research station. And here it is!'

Rounding the bend, they saw it: a big wooden house on stilts, overlooking the river.

'There's a lake on the other side, 'Leon explained, steering the boat to a jetty and stopping the engine. 'Right now, the house is on dry land. But during the highwater season, for about three months, only those tall stilts keep it safely above the water. Then, when the river and lake-waters actually meet, we can take the boat right up to the front door!

'But we're in the "rivers falling" season now,' he reminded them, leaping out onto the jetty. He tied the boat securely to a post with a rope that was fastened there and then turned his warm smile on his passengers. 'Come with me and meet the others.'

They followed him up a wooden staircase and into a casually cluttered living-room/office area. It was furnished with a couch and several wicker chairs, but also two computer workstations.

A dark, handsome man with a neatly trimmed beard was seated in front of one of the computers. He got to his feet as they entered. Leon introduced him to everyone as Dr Carlos Benevides.

'We read your study of the social life of botos,' Craig said, shaking Carlos firmly by the hand. 'Wonderful work!'

'Thank you,' the Venezuelan scientist replied, with a warm smile. 'I myself have enjoyed following your travels via the Dolphin Universe website. I feel as if we are friends already!'

'Come along, we can talk in the kitchen,' Leon urged. 'I'm dying for a cup of coffee!'

'Oh, me, too!' Gina exclaimed.

'And me,' said Dr Taylor, perking up a little. He mopped his perspiring face with a large handkerchief.

Jody didn't care about coffee, but she followed the others to the kitchen.

'This is our other resident researcher,' Leon said as they entered the large room. 'Julie Baker, who came here all the way from England, two years ago, to study the boto.'

Julie was a young woman, who wore a pair of gold-rimmed glasses. Her brown hair was cut into a neat, short bob which framed her attractive, rounded features. She turned away from the stove to greet them. 'How was your journey?' she asked, after introductions had been made. Her eyes fell on Juan and she grinned. 'I see you picked up another passenger along the way!'

'We had to rescue Ocho from a net,' Juan told her.

Her face clouded. 'Is he all right?' she asked anxiously.

'Last seen swimming off at top speed to find his mama,' Leon replied, smiling.

Julie gave a sigh of relief. She turned back to the stove and plucked something from a simmering pot. Surprised, Jody saw that she now held a very large baby's bottle.

Julie tested the temperature of the milk by shaking a few drops onto her wrist. She nodded in satisfaction. 'Well, I'm off to nurse the baby,' she said. 'Anybody want to come?'

'I do!' said Juan.

His eagerness made Jody suspicious. 'What kind of a baby is it?' she asked.

Julie smiled mysteriously. 'It's a little boy . . .

manatee,' she drawled, and laughed at the looks on their faces.

'A manatee!' Sean exclaimed. 'You mean, a sea-cow?'

'We've got them in Florida,' Jimmy piped up.

Julie nodded. 'Yes, I know. But the South American manatee is much smaller than its relatives in Florida.'

'What happened to his mother?' Brittany asked, frowning with concern.

'Killed by a hunter,' Juan told her.

Jody gasped in horror. 'Aren't manatees protected here?' she asked. In Florida, she knew, the manatee was an endangered species.

'There's supposed to be a ban on hunting them,' Julie explained. 'But it's hard to enforce. They're supposed to be delicious, and, of course, the local people don't get many chances to eat meat.'

'At least we managed to save this one,' Juan said.

Jody looked at him, surprised and respectful. 'Did *you* save him?' she asked.

'Not me myself,' he said quickly, looking embarrassed at the misunderstanding.

'It was an American researcher named Buddy Watkins who found the manatee calf,' Julie explained. 'Juan was here when the calf was brought in, and he's been an enormous help.'

Juan shrugged shyly as the young Englishwoman turned a dazzling smile on him.

'We named the little calf Buddy after his rescuer,' Julie went on. 'Buddy Watkins did more than just find him - he also donated nearly two thousand dollars to build a special concrete tank so we can keep little Buddy safe and look after him until he grows up.' She moved towards the door. 'But that's enough talk - Buddy wants his milk - come and meet him yourselves!'

6

A grey, whiskered snout poked out of the water. Tiny, deepset eyes blinked up at them.

'Hello, Buddy,' Julie said softly. 'Hungry? Here's some new friends, to help feed you.'

Jody's eyes widened at the sight of the strange-looking creature. It had a fat, blubbery grey body rather like a seal's, which ended in a wide, flat tail. The stubby little flippers looked like they'd been stuck on to the shapeless body as an afterthought.

'Wow, he's so ugly, he's actually cute!' Brittany exclaimed.

Jody laughed. She completely agreed.

'Would one of you boys like to have a go at feeding Buddy?' Julie asked, turning to the twins. She smiled apologetically. 'I'm sorry, but I can't remember which of you is which!'

'I'm Jimmy, and I'm the eldest,' Jimmy announced, pointing at his chest. 'So I get to go first!'

Sean frowned but didn't object; he was used to letting his brother take the lead.

'Don't worry,' said Julie, with a glance around at them all. 'Everyone will have a chance to feed Buddy while you're here. He takes four bottles a day!'

Jimmy let Julie show him where to stand. 'Hold the bottle tightly with both hands,' she cautioned him. 'Buddy is pretty strong now, and he really pulls away at the teat!'

At the sight of the feeding bottle, the hungry young manatee reared up out of the water. He seemed very big for a baby, well over a metre long, and quite fat.

With a soft grunt, Buddy latched on to the bottle right away and began to suck.

'Wow,' said Jimmy, bracing himself. 'This guy really is hungry!'

Jody couldn't help but smile as she watched Buddy feed. After a few moments, he closed his little eyes, looking utterly blissful. His slit-like nostrils opened and closed as he breathed.

'He wasn't always such a good eater,' Julie told them. 'When we first tried to feed him, the milk just dribbled out of his mouth. We didn't think he would survive. But then we made contact with a manatee expert in Brazil. She told us that ordinary milk wouldn't do for Buddy. He needed a lactose-free formula with some extra nutrients and fatty acids that would be closer to his mother's milk. After we put him onto the special formula, he finally started to thrive.'

'How much longer will you need to bottle-feed him?' Jody wondered.

'For at least another year,' Julie replied. 'He's already a year old, but manatees stay with their mothers for quite a long time. Even after we wean him, we'll want to keep a close eye on him for a few more months, until we feel sure he's fit enough to be released.'

'What do full-grown manatees eat?' Brittany asked.

'They're herbivores,' Julie said. 'So just plants.'

'All this talk about food is making me hungry,'

Sean said plaintively, rubbing his stomach with one hand.

Julie laughed. 'It looks like Buddy is nearly finished with his bottle,' she said. 'Let's go back to the kitchen and see what sort of tasty goodies Leon brought back from his trip to the big city!'

November 8 – night, research station – River Orinoco, Venezuela.

Uh-oh, Dad really put his foot in it with Brittany! Over dinner he said something about 'Brittany's young admirer' – meaning Juan. Well, Brittany went bright red! Leon said that Juan probably thought she was one of the encantados.

That means 'enchanted' in Spanish – but to the people who live along the river, it has another meaning. According to Leon, the local people say there are two kinds of botos. There are the ordinary ones – the animals – and the encantados. *Encantados can change their form and come onto dry land, looking like pale, fair-haired, pink-skinned people. And it is well-known that anyone who meets an encantado is bound to fall in love . . .*

Brittany tried to look as if she didn't care, but she couldn't help blushing.

Of course, Jimmy noticed, and started teasing her about her 'boyfriend'. Luckily Mom made him quit before things got out of hand.

It's too bad, because Juan is really nice, and I think Brittany thinks so, too. I noticed she was talking to him just before he left. Why shouldn't they be friends? But now she will probably freeze him out, just to keep from getting teased by my monkey-brothers . . .

Next morning, they all rose early again, before the sun was up.

As they gathered in the kitchen, Leon explained that they'd need to split into two groups to explore the lake in smaller boats. He would pilot one, and Julie the other.

'Boys in one boat, girls in the other,' Jimmy suggested.

'That suits me,' Brittany quickly agreed as Jody nodded.

So it was settled: Gina, Jody and Brittany would go with Julie, while Craig, the twins and Dr Taylor would be in Leon's boat.

'Do you do most of your research on the lake or in the river?' Gina asked Julie as they set off in her canoe in the grey light of early morning.

'Both places,' Julie replied, dipping her paddle into the water and sending the little boat gliding easily along. She went on, 'But they're easier to keep tabs on here – out in the river, they disappear for days. Also, at this time of year, the lake provides a nursery pool where mothers and their calves stay, along with a few female helpers.'

A nursery pool! Jody's breath caught with excitement. 'Does that mean we're going to see some babies – I mean, calves?' she asked.

Julie smiled at her as she paddled the canoe. 'I hope so!' she replied. 'Botos are usually born when the rivers are starting to fall. Around here, that's September or October. When the water levels drop the fish are more concentrated, so the botos don't have to travel very far to find food.'

'We got to see some baby bottlenose dolphins being born when we were in the Bahamas,' Brittany offered shyly. 'That was pretty cool.'

'Lucky you!' Julie exclaimed warmly. 'I've never seen a boto calf being born, but Posy can't have been more than a few minutes old when I first met her.'

'Who's Posy?' Gina asked, looking up from checking her video camera.

Julie smiled. 'That's Posy right there,' she said, nodding towards her right.

They all looked where Julie had indicated. Gina raised her video camera and began recording.

'Oh, how sweet!' Jody cried. There in the water – or, more accurately, *on* the water, only a few feet away from the canoe, she saw the young boto. The top of her head – the melon – was dark grey, and so was a strip running along her back, including the low dorsal ridge, but the rest of her body was pale pink. Like every other dolphin Jody had ever seen, this one, too, seemed to be smiling.

Jody felt the strongest urge to scoop Posy into her arms and hug her!

Then the strangeness of the sight struck her. How could she see so much of an animal that spent most of its time underwater? What on earth was she lying on? Was she stranded? 'What's Posy doing out of the water?' she asked anxiously. 'Is she all right?'

'I should hope so,' Julie replied, chuckling. 'Posy's lying on top of her mum!'

As Julie spoke, there was a ripple in the water. It

spread out around Posy, and the young boto began to rise up. The bubblegum-pink body of another, bigger, boto was pushing her up. Now the big boto breathed out with an explosive, coughing sound.

'Meet Valentine,' Julie said, waving her hand towards the newcomer.

Valentine turned her head to inspect the people in the boat.

'Yes, it's me, Val,' Julie said, leaning out to speak to her. 'I've brought a few friends to meet you and your beautiful baby!'

In reply, Valentine reared up in the water. This sudden movement threw Posy off her back, and the calf thrashed awkwardly for a few moments, her flippers paddling wildly.

Valentine immediately dropped back, all her attention focused on her calf. She nudged Posy gently.

Jody watched the mother and calf rub against each other in the water. She sighed with relief to see that nothing was wrong.

'Oh, dear, Val,' said Julie, shaking her head ruefully. 'You must try to remember that you're a mother now – and that your baby can't always keep up with you!'

'Is this her first calf?' Gina asked, still focusing her camcorder on the scene in the lake.

'We can't be certain,' Julie replied. 'But after observing them together practically every day for two months, I'm convinced of it! I think Valentine is still pretty young, too – for all her size!'

'But won't the other female botos teach Val what to do?' Jody asked. She knew that bottlenose and other types of dolphins were nearly always helped by one or more 'aunts' during and after they gave birth.

'I think botos aren't as social as marine dolphins,' her mother told her. 'I've read that the boto is quite a solitary animal.'

'Actually, our research has shown that's not quite true,' Julie replied. 'Earlier researchers on the Amazon River thought that, but now we know that botos do live in stable social groups. They spend most of their time in groups of up to five or six – at least the ones in the Orinoco do! And the females help each other out, like all dolphins, everywhere.'

She smiled at Jody. 'So Jody's question was spot

on. Unfortunately for Valentine, though, there were a lot of births this season. So all the females we might have expected to play auntie to Posy are busy looking after calves of their own!'

Jody watched as Valentine and Posy swam away together, sticking so close to each other now that they seemed glued together!

'How many more babies are there?' Brittany asked.

Julie picked up her paddle again and the canoe began to glide along, directed by her firm, strong strokes. 'There've been five calves born in the lake this season,' she replied. 'But of course the ones born last year are still with their mothers. Botos don't grow up too quickly,' she explained. 'It's a very close relationship. Calves can stay with their mothers for up to three years. They–'

Julie broke off with a yell. The canoe lurched and rocked heavily to one side.

Jody clutched anxiously at her seat, afraid they were about to overturn.

'What's going on?' asked Gina, cradling the video camera protectively.

'Something's got my paddle,' Julie gasped. She was hanging on to her end with all her might. Something

Something's trying to capsize our canoe!

unseen in the water was trying to tug it away.

'Oh, no!' Brittany cried, her voice a high, thin wail. 'We'll be stuck!'

All of a sudden, the paddle came free as whatever had been holding it under the water let go. The canoe rocked wildly again as Julie fell back in her seat.

A familiar, soft coughing sound attracted Jody's attention. Looking over the side of the boat she saw a shiny grey melon, the blow-hole open as it breathed.

Moments later, the whole head pushed through into the air. The boto opened its beak, revealing the long rows of sharp, dangerous-looking teeth.

'He's laughing at us,' said Julie. 'Ocho, you bad boy, scaring us like that!' She tried to sound stern, but laughter won out.

Ocho shook his head back and forth, watching them intently all the while.

'Ocho! You're all right,' Jody said happily. She leaned over the side, wondering if she dared reach out to stroke him. 'Where's your mother?' she asked.

'Over there,' said Julie, pointing. 'Here's Viva, coming after him now. I'll bet after yesterday's little adventure she doesn't want to let her son out of her sight!'

Jody turned eagerly to look. Sure enough, here came a large pink dolphin, heading straight for Ocho. In response, Ocho turned and scooted in her direction, doing an enthusiastic belly-flop.

Water splashed everywhere, showering down on them, and the little boat rocked wildly on the wave created by the excited young boto. They all watched as Ocho greeted Viva by rubbing himself against her.

Then Jody noticed something that made her gasp with surprise. There was a small, greyish calf pressed close against Viva's other side. 'Look, Julie,' she said, pointing. 'Whose baby is that? Is Viva babysitting?'

'That's Viva's new calf,' Julie replied. 'We've called him Cinco. He was born just five weeks ago.'

Jody gasped. She saw her own surprise mirrored on her mother's face.

'How is that possible?' Gina asked. 'If Ocho is only just over a year old . . .'

'That's another difference between botos and marine dolphins,' Julie replied. 'Most mammals, including marine dolphins, can't get pregnant if they're still producing milk for their calf. Botos are unusual in that they can,' she explained. 'This is because their pregnancies last quite a long time – nearly a year. So by the time the new calf is born, the older one would have been weaned, so wouldn't compete with the newborn for their mother's milk. Though Ocho was still feeding from Viva when she got pregnant with Cinco, he was weaned several months before his little brother finally appeared.'

Julie pushed the paddle back into the water and steered the boat around the dolphins. She went on, 'Ocho can hunt for fish and feed himself now. But he's not as skilled as an adult. He still needs a lot of help from his mother.'

Jody gazed into the lake at the little family of three. Now she understood why Ocho had been on his own and had got trapped. 'But Viva can't always help him, because she's got the new baby to look after,' she said slowly.

'That's right,' Julie agreed. 'That's it exactly!'

'Well, then, Ocho is really lucky he's got someone like Juan to look out for him,' Brittany said unexpectedly.

Jody turned to look at her in surprise. Brittany flushed self-consciously. 'And Leon and Julie and

Carlos, too, of course,' she added quickly. Then she shrugged, the old, defensive, bored expression returning to her face. 'Not that *I* care,' she drawled, turning away.

But Jody could tell that, no matter how Brittany might try to pretend otherwise, the charm of the river dolphins was working its spell on her.

7

November 9 – late afternoon – research station.

No time to have breakfast before going out on the lake this morning, so when we got back we had a huge brunch, followed by a siesta. Even me, and I never take naps! But a siesta makes sense if you're getting up at 5 a.m. . . .

I'm finding out about all the ways the botos are in danger – it's really frightening! But if everyone in Juan's village feels the way he does, then I just know things will get better!

And speaking of Juan – I've got to run! He came over to invite us all to his house for dinner . . .

Jody put her diary away and hurried to join everyone at the front of the house.

'I'll come along a little later, to bring you back here by boat,' Leon told them. 'But we thought you all might enjoy a walk through the rainforest, while it's still light enough.'

'That sounds great,' Craig agreed.

Soon, they were following Juan away from the research centre, into the deep, green foliage of the rainforest.

The path was quite narrow in places, and Jody couldn't help wondering nervously about snakes and spiders as she walked. Her brothers had gleefully informed everyone that Venezuela was home to the world's largest tarantulas!

Yet it was also a place of almost magical beauty, with something new and different to see at every turn. Overhead, monkeys were screaming and calling to each other, and so were birds.

Dr Taylor kept stopping to peer up into the branches, trying to identify the birds.

While the younger members of the party moved ahead, following the trail more quickly, Craig and Gina hung back, making sure Dr Taylor didn't fall so far behind that he got lost.

Juan ran back and forth, utterly at home, keeping watch over his guests. He was especially attentive to Brittany, warning her whenever there was a possibility she might stumble, pulling trailing vines and low branches back out of her way, and always murmuring politely in Spanish and gazing at her with adoring brown eyes.

Jody thought Brittany was looking a little flushed. She couldn't tell if she was pleased or embarrassed by Juan's constant attention.

Unfortunately, Jody wasn't the only one who had noticed.

Jimmy punched Sean lightly on the arm. 'Ooh, look, Brittany's got a boyfriend,' he said making a silly face.

'Shut up, you stupid little brat,' Brittany snapped.

Jimmy's eyes lit up with mischievous delight at getting a response from his victim. 'Brittany's got a boyfriend, Brittany's got a boyfriend!' he crowed.

Brittany went fiery red. 'They're silly apes - don't listen to them,' she begged Juan.

'Oh, yeah? You're the ape,' Jimmy replied,

scowling. He turned to Juan. 'How can you stand to have a girlfriend as ugly as Brittany?'

Juan gazed back at Jimmy in astonishment. 'How can you say she is ugly? Brittany is the most beautiful girl I have ever seen!'

Sean hooted at this.

Jimmy shrieked, 'Oooh, he's in luuurve!'

'Stop it, you two!' Jody said sharply. 'Or you'll be in trouble.'

'I don't understand,' Juan said, confused by the peculiar way Jimmy hooted the word. 'What is "luuurve"?'

Jimmy laughed. 'Your boyfriend is a little slow, Brittany!'

'He's not my boyfriend!' Brittany yelled. 'So just shut up about it!' After saying that, she charged away down the trail.

Juan hesitated a moment, looking unhappy. Then he hurried after Brittany just as Craig caught up to them.

'What's going on here?' he asked, casting a suspicious glance at the twins.

'Nothing,' said Sean, looking innocent.

'They were teasing Juan and Brittany,' Jody

said when her dad looked at her.

'I only said the truth,' Jimmy declared.

'That's enough,' Craig said firmly. 'Whatever you were saying, it wasn't making Juan happy. I won't have that. He's our host, remember? No teasing! And leave Brittany alone, too. I don't want to have to tell you about this again, understand?'

Jimmy shrugged and sighed while Sean nodded meekly.

They reached Juan's village a few minutes later.

The simple wooden houses all had thatched roofs and were raised on stilts to keep them safe and dry in the rainy season. Juan pointed out his school, a larger version of the houses, and explained, 'Only a little while ago we had to paddle to school in canoes!'

Jody was surprised. 'Does everyone have a canoe?'

Juan nodded. 'Oh, yes. In the rainy season, it's the only way to get around.'

'Kind of like bicycles, back home,' Sean suggested. 'You have canoes and boats, and in Florida, we have bicycles and cars!'

As they walked through the village, Jody noticed

some little girls watching them. When she turned to smile at them they burst into giggles and ran away.

'Here's my house,' Juan announced, leading the way in.

Inside it was spacious and airy; almost cool after the close, stifling heat outside. Juan's parents, Cecilia and Mario, greeted them in Spanish, with warm smiles and offers of fresh guava juice to drink.

Juan introduced his little sister, Maria. She was an adorable little girl dressed all in pink, hiding shyly behind her mother and peeking out at the strangers.

The juice was delicious. But after she had finished it, Jody couldn't help feeling a little bored as her parents and Juan's chatted away in Spanish. She noticed that Dr Taylor, sitting in a corner, seemed to be nodding off. Her brothers were fidgeting. Jimmy had that look on his face that promised trouble.

Luckily, Gina noticed, too. She spoke to Cecilia, who, in turn, spoke to Juan.

Juan nodded, then turned to Jody, Brittany and the twins. 'Let's go outside and explore for a while, before dinner,' he said.

Jody, Jimmy and Sean followed him eagerly. Only Brittany did not move.

'Come on, Britt,' Jody said.

The other girl shook her head. 'No, thanks, I'd rather stay here.' She avoided looking at Juan.

Jody shrugged. 'Suit yourself.'

As soon as they were outside, Sean and Jimmy shot off as if fired from a gun. 'Race you to the river!' Sean cried.

Juan hung back with Jody, walking more slowly. Turning to her unhappily he burst out, 'Why doesn't Brittany like me?'

Jody bit her lip. 'I'm sure she does, really.'

Juan shook his head. 'You heard her – she said I wasn't her friend. And when I tried to help her, in the forest, she told me to leave her alone!'

'She was embarrassed. It's all the twins' fault,' Jody struggled to explain.

'But why should she be embarrassed? Why did she say I was not her friend?' Juan asked unhappily.

'She didn't say that,' Jody objected. She frowned, remembering. 'She said you weren't her *boyfriend*.'

Juan shrugged. 'So? I am a boy, a boy-friend. What is the difference?'

'There *is* a difference,' Jody told him. 'Friend means *amigo*. Boyfriend . . .' she paused, uncertain of the term in Spanish. 'Well, a boyfriend is different,' she went on, awkwardly. 'That's someone you go out with . . . who you like in a special way . . . well, who you might want to marry.'

Juan stared at her in astonishment. 'But I am too young to marry,' he objected. 'And Brittany . . . do girls get married at thirteen in your country?'

'No, of course not!' Jody said laughing. 'Jimmy and Sean were just giving her a hard time . . .'

Juan nodded as he understood. 'They were saying I am her *novio*, her boyfriend. She doesn't like that. OK. But, Jody, tell me: will Brittany let me be her friend? Or does she hate me too much?'

'I don't think she hates you at all,' Jody said earnestly. She was pleased to see the unhappiness vanish from Juan's face.

They had reached the river. There they found Sean and Jimmy at the centre of a group of children all gazing out at group of playful, acrobatic dolphins.

Jody immediately saw that these were not botos but tucuxi. She counted nine of them jumping and diving. They weren't just playing – they were

The Tucuxi – getting ready for dinner!

hunting. The flat, silvery bodies of fish also jumped clear out of the water, as if in imitation of the leaping dolphins which chased them. The group of nine dolphins had encountered a school of fish, and now they were working together, helping each other round up and catch their dinner. She watched them work, fascinated, and wished she had a camera.

A call from further down the river made them look around. It was Leon approaching in *Tonina*. As she waved back at him, Jody noticed that the dolphins were starting to scatter.

Dinner was a delicious meal of grilled fish and tasty pancakes filled with a mixture of chopped vegetables grown in the family garden.

As they ate, the visitors learned a little more about life in the village.

It was a simple, old-fashioned place, far from the modern world, without mains electricity or indoor plumbing. There were no televisions or telephones, no computers or cars. It was very different from the world Jody had always known! But Juan's parents felt that life was good, because the river and the forest provided well, and there was plenty of food for everyone.

'And one day soon we will have electricity,' Juan announced proudly. 'Then we get all the good, modern things we want: a refrigerator for Mama, a chainsaw for Papa, maybe a television – or even a computer for me!'

'The government has plans to build a dam and a hydro-electric plant,' Leon explained. 'It is said to be necessary, and the people certainly want it. But it will mean big, big changes, especially for the rainforest. What's good for the people won't be good for wildlife.'

'We don't want to do anything bad to the dolphins,' Juan said anxiously.

Leon smiled at him. 'No, of course not. But a dam will change the landscape; will change the dolphins' habitat. These are problems we need to think about. We need to learn from what has happened in other parts of the world, and not repeat the same mistakes. Fortunately, we still have some time to make plans. Hopefully, the work we're doing at the research station will help.'

As Leon spoke, something dropped from the rafters onto the table-top. It was a brown furry creature the size of a basketball. Squealing, it launched itself straight at Jody!

8

Jody gasped as a small warm creature landed on her chest. She felt something snuggling beneath her chin, and a pair of tiny arms clutched her around the neck.

'A monkey!' Jimmy exclaimed. He and Sean jumped up from the table and came to have a look.

'Oh, Chuchi, you bad thing!' Juan exclaimed, hurrying over to Jody. 'It's my sister's pet woolly monkey,' he explained.

Jody laughed. Her heart was still pounding hard from the sudden fright, but now that she knew what it was, she didn't mind. She stroked its soft fur, enjoying the way it cuddled against her.

'What an adorable little monkey!' Brittany cried. 'Oh, Jody, please can I hold it?'

'You should put it down at once!' Dr Taylor exclaimed. 'It's probably crawling with parasites!'

Gently unwrapping the small, warm creature from her neck, Jody pulled the monkey down to have a look at it. 'Oh, isn't she sweet?' she exclaimed. Sad-looking brown eyes blinked up at her out of a furry face.

Eventually, Jody handed the little monkey over to Brittany who was hovering excitedly with her hands out. She expected Chuchi to protest, but the monkey seemed quite happy to go to someone else. In fact, she cuddled up in Brittany's arms as if she was her long-lost best friend.

Brittany's face glowed as she held the little creature close. 'Oh, it's so sweet,' she murmured. 'The cutest little thing I've ever seen!'

'You can keep her,' Juan said.

Startled, Brittany looked right at him. Jody thought it was the first time she'd done so since the twins had teased them in the forest. 'But – you said this was your sister's pet?' she asked.

Juan shrugged. 'Well, yes, but Maria is too little to look after a pet, really. If she misses Chuchi, I can catch another monkey for her, any time. There are lots of them in the forest.'

Brittany looked dazzled. She drew in a deep breath. 'Oh, gosh! That's the most wonderful present anyone–'

'Hey, if she gets to have a monkey, can we have a tarantula?' Jimmy demanded of his parents.

'*Two* tarantulas,' Sean put in. 'One each!'

'Heavens!' murmured Dr Taylor unhappily.

'Absolutely not,' said Craig firmly. 'Nobody is taking any animals away from here. I'm sorry, Brittany, but you can't possibly keep that monkey.'

'Oh, please!' she cried. 'It wouldn't be much trouble! Look how tiny she is - and so tame! I promise I'd look after her myself. I'd keep her in my cabin–'

'*Our* cabin,' Jody reminded her. She liked the idea, and turned hopefully to her father. 'Please, Dad,' she began.

'Absolutely not,' said Gina in her no-nonsense voice.

'Juan, I'm surprised at you,' said Leon gently. 'After

all the times we've talked about how wrong it is to capture animals and take them away from their natural habitat, how can you suggest such a thing?'

Juan looked embarrassed. He swallowed hard, and tried to argue. 'Of course the wildlife trade is wrong – but this is different!' he exclaimed. 'Woolly monkeys aren't an endangered species – and Brittany is my friend – I'm sure she would look after Chuchi well!'

'Of course I would,' Brittany said, holding the monkey close to her. She frowned, beginning to pout, but kept her temper under control. 'Oh, *please*. I promise she wouldn't be any trouble!'

'That's not the point,' Gina said gently. 'Think about Chuchi. This is where she lives. She's free to come and go as she pleases. She can run back to the forest whenever she likes. It would be cruel to keep her cooped up on board a boat.'

'And think of this,' Leon put in. 'Many people want only *one* monkey or one tarantula or rare bird – but add all those people up, and they are a huge market which keeps the cruel and dangerous international trade in wildlife going. The only way to stop it is to refuse to allow *any* animals to be taken.' He looked around. 'Understand?'

Jody nodded slowly. So did her brothers, looking very solemn.

'I'm sorry,' Juan said quietly.

Brittany's lower lip was thrust out stubbornly, but she didn't argue.

'I'm sorry,' Juan said again, this time to Brittany. 'I wasn't thinking . . . Chuchi will have to stay here. But . . . you can pet her and play with her as much as you like, for as long as you're here. She'll be your friend, just like I am.'

Jody, used to Brittany's long, silent sulks, was astonished when Brittany looked up, met Juan's eyes, and even managed a little smile. 'Thanks,' she murmured, and then lowered her head to cuddle the monkey.

November 9 – late at night
Juan told us an amazing story after dinner. He said one of the fishermen in the village had gotten angry when he found a boto tangled in his net. It was still alive, but, instead of setting it free, the fisherman killed it with his spear. His wife was expecting a baby, and when the baby was born, it looked just like a dolphin! It died

after a few days. Everyone knew this was the fisherman's punishment for killing a magical boto. Now, nobody in the village would dare *to kill a boto.*

Juan swears this is true – his parents agreed. Everyone in the village had seen the baby. Juan said the baby had a hole in the top of her head, just like a dolphin.

I could hardly believe it. Yet, if Juan saw it himself . . . ?

Mom told me later that the baby might have been suffering from something called 'spina bifida'. She said sometimes babies are born too badly deformed to live, and they might well resemble dolphins.

Well, whatever the reason, it's lucky for the boto that local people think it's unlucky to kill them.

Jody woke early the next morning, feeling terrible. Her arms prickled and itched. So did her chest and neck, and her back.

Wriggling uncomfortably, Jody groaned and opened her eyes. She looked at her arms and gasped in horror. They were covered in hard, pink bumps. In fact, as she realised when she sat up and examined herself more closely, she had the little swellings all over her body – and they itched like mad!

Across the room, Brittany was thrashing around in her bed. Now she gave a cry and sat up. 'I've got bed-bugs!'

Jody jumped up. She pulled back the sheet and stared closely at the mattress. But nothing moved there. She didn't see so much as a single flea.

'Maybe they're mosquito bites,' Jody said doubtfully.

'Mosquito bites were never as bad as this!' Brittany exclaimed, scratching fiercely at herself.

Jody quickly put her clothes on. 'Let's go ask Julie,' she suggested. 'Maybe she'll have something to stop the itching.'

'Oh, I hope so,' Brittany said as she also scrambled to get dressed. 'Otherwise, I just know I'm going to *die*.'

They found Julie in the kitchen, brewing a pot of tea. Craig was making coffee, while Leon was cracking eggs into a bowl and Gina was searching for something in the fridge.

'Julie, look!' Brittany exclaimed, stretching out her arms. 'We're absolutely covered in these horrible, itchy bites! Do you know what they are?'

Julie put the cover on the teapot and came over to

have a look. 'Hmm, looks like chiggers. Were you by any chance cuddling a monkey yesterday?'

'Yes!' Jody gasped.

'Well, that's the answer, then. Cute as they are, monkeys are crawling with little, biting chiggers. They're almost too tiny to be seen, but they itch like mad.'

'Do you have some medicine we could put on the bites?' Jody asked hopefully.

Julie shook her head regretfully. 'I don't think there is anything, really . . . Unless,' she brightened. 'I know! Nail polish! Put a dab on each bite and let it harden.'

'I'll try anything!' Brittany exclaimed. Then she frowned. 'But I left my nail polish back on board *Dolphin Dreamer* – I never thought I'd need it here! Do you have some, Julie?'

But Julie shook her head. 'Sorry. My last reserves of make-up ran out about six months ago!'

'I'm afraid I didn't bring any along, either,' Gina said. 'I'm sorry, girls.'

'What are we going to do?' Brittany groaned.

Just then, Juan came in. '*Buenas dias*,' he called cheerfully. Then, as he caught sight of

Jody and Brittany's miserable faces, his expression became concerned. 'Something is wrong?' he asked anxiously.

'We've been bitten to pieces!' Jody exclaimed. 'Chuchi was covered with chiggers . . . and now we are, as well. And we don't know how to stop them itching!'

'I think I do,' said Juan. 'Come with me.'

Jody glanced at her mother, who nodded permission.

They followed him out of the building. He led them away from the river, into the forest.

'Are we going to your house?' Brittany asked.

Juan shook his head. 'There is a plant that grows in the forest. It will stop the itching,' he told them. He left the trail, heading deeper into the darkness of the forest. He walked slowly, often stopping to peer carefully into the lush undergrowth.

Jody chewed her lip, trying not to scratch the bites. She knew she would be even more uncomfortable if they got infected.

At last, Juan gave a low cry of triumph. He bent down and carefully broke off two thick, fleshy leaves, each one as big as a man's hand. He handed one to Jody and one to Brittany. 'Break it apart gently and squeeze a bit of the insides onto each bite,' he told them.

Jody tried it on her arm. The thick sap that oozed out felt cool. The bites felt better immediately as she spread the cool juice onto them. As it dried, the itching stopped.

'It's like magic!' Brittany cried. 'But I can't reach the ones on my back . . .'

'We'll help each other, back in our room,' Jody

Relief!

said. She looked at Juan. 'Will this one leaf be enough? We've got a *lot* of bites!'

'Better each take another one, then,' Juan said. He bent down again and got two more of the big, thick, dark green leaves.

'Thank you, Juan, you're a lifesaver!' Brittany exclaimed, giving him a brilliant smile.

Juan shook his head, looking shy and pleased. 'Not me,' he replied. 'Thank the rainforest!'

When Jody walked with Brittany into the kitchen for the second time – feeling sticky and bumpy but blessedly itch-free – she was startled to find her parents, the twins and Leon all packed and seemingly ready to go. 'What about breakfast?' she asked, dismayed. Her tummy was rumbling!

'Don't worry, I've made something to take along this time,' Leon said. 'To see the dolphins, it's vital to make an early start. They all disappear once the sun gets high. For a change, we're going out on the river today.'

'But Carlos and I are staying here,' Julie said. 'Carlos has to finish writing a grant application, and I need to monitor the botos in the lake, as usual. I promised Dr Taylor I'd take him with me, to see if we could get a look at the hoatzins.'

Sean gasped. 'The dinosaur bird! They have claws on the ends of their wings, and they hiss like lizards if you scare them! Oh, I want to see them, too!'

'Me, too!' added Jimmy. 'They sound really cool – Dr T. was telling us about them!'

'Dr T.?' Craig repeated, arching his brows quizzically.

'It's a much cooler name than "Dr Taylor",' Sean explained.

'I'm not sure he'd agree,' said Craig, grinning.

'Please, can we go with Julie and Dr T.?' Jimmy begged.

'It's OK with me,' Julie said, smiling.

'If you're sure,' said Gina, smiling back. Then she nodded. 'OK, boys. But you're not to get up to any mischief! Do whatever Julie tells you, and don't bother Dr Taylor!'

'Thanks, Mom,' said Sean.

'We'll be little angels,' added Jimmy, with a wicked grin.

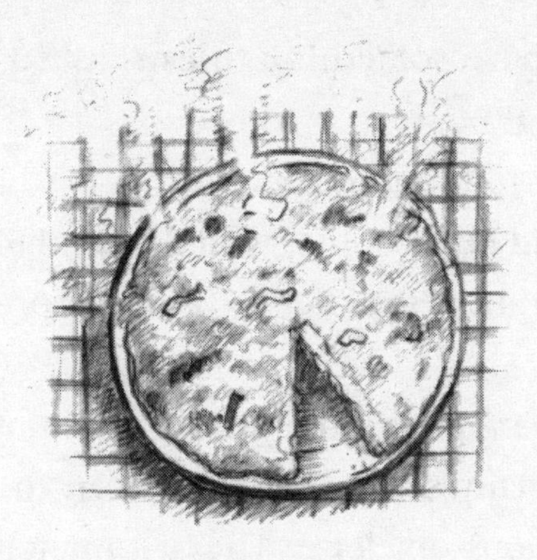

9

Juan followed Brittany, the McGraths and Leon down to the dock where *Tonina* was tied up.

'*Por favor, Leon*,' he said shyly. 'I come too?'

Leon raised an eyebrow. 'Don't you have school to go to?'

'Not on a Saturday!' Juan objected.

Leon looked surprised. 'Of course, it's Saturday!' he exclaimed. 'I've lost track of the days . . . yes, sure, come along with us, Juan!' he replied, smiling.

As soon as they were all on board, Leon started the motor and they chugged away.

'Could I have something to eat?' asked Brittany. 'I'm starving!'

'Me, too,' Jody agreed.

'Sure,' said Leon. 'Gina, would you mind serving up? I wouldn't say no to a slice of tortilla, myself!'

To Jody's surprise, the 'tortilla' was not the flat pancake usually served with Mexican food, but a thick, delicious omelette. They all munched away happily for a few minutes until Juan shouted out, '*Mira! Mira los botos*!'

Even Jody understood that: Look at the botos!

Jody caught her breath at the sight of a flash of pink, and a waving flipper as one boto slipped beneath the water right beside the boat. Another one shot past, chasing a fish.

Leon shut off the engine. In the sudden silence, they could hear the slap of waves against *Tonina's* wooden sides.

Now they could hear gentle, sighing, coughing sounds as, all around them, the botos surfaced for a moment to breathe before slipping beneath the water again.

'They're having their breakfast, too,' Craig

remarked as Gina scrambled to get the camcorder into operation.

Jody gazed out at the water, catching brief glimpses of grey and pink as the botos moved through the water. Their closeness was thrilling, but also frustrating. She kept wanting to see more!

'You'll notice how different their hunting style is from that of the tucuxi,' Leon said. 'The tucuxi tend to hunt in groups, rounding up whole shoals of fish to feed on. The botos go chasing after individual fish instead. Often, the boto will go fishing in very shallow water, which would be hard, if not impossible, for the other kinds of dolphin.'

Jody remembered stories she had heard about whales getting stranded. 'Do they ever get stuck?' she asked.

'It's very rare,' Leon replied. He frowned thoughtfully. 'I suppose it must happen sometimes, but, you see, botos are so flexible and strong that even if they chase a fish right onto a sandbank, they can wriggle back into the water without too much trouble.'

He went on, 'I have seen them get stuck in water-holes, sometimes, if the channel connecting it to the river completely dries up. But it's not a problem, as there's plenty of fish to eat. They just have to wait until the land floods again before they can move on.'

'Oh, wow, look at this one! He wants to be a star!' Gina exclaimed.

They all looked where she was pointing her camera. Sure enough, one of the botos had abandoned fishing for the moment to spy-hop. He was taking a good look at the people on board *Tonina*, and giving them a good look at him in return.

'Wow, he's huge!' Jody said. The dolphin seemed to be smiling right at her, and she couldn't help smiling back.

The other dolphins were harder to see. They showed themselves only briefly, in bits and pieces, as they darted after fish.

'They're too busy to come and say hello,' Leon sighed.

After fifteen or twenty minutes, the botos began to disappear. They'd had their breakfast; now they would go somewhere else to rest for a while.

When the last of the botos had gone, Leon started up the engine again and they motored slowly along.

Jody hung over the side, gazing at the dark brown river, hoping to see more botos. The day hadn't started to heat up yet, so they should still be active.

A splashing caught her attention.

'Look, there's one,' said Gina, raising the camcorder just as a boto surfaced beside the boat. Jody caught sight of a dark, bubblegum-pink body before it went under again. The colour made her think of Valentine.

The boto swam in a big circle and approached the boat again. This time it reared up in the water, giving them a good look before splashing heavily down.

'That looks like Valentine,' Leon said, sounding surprised.

Jody caught her breath. 'Then where's Posy?' she asked. Staring into the water she could see no sign of the young calf.

'Maybe I'm wrong,' Leon said. He frowned, gazing over the side at the bright pink boto who kept swimming back and forth, going away from the boat and then returning. 'It can be hard to recognise individuals, especially the way they change colour . . . No, I'm sure Valentine and Posy would stay in the lake. There's plenty of fish there, and Posy's still too young to travel far. It must be another dolphin.'

'She looks like Valentine to me,' Juan said, staring intently at the boto.

'Whoever it is seems to know the boat,' Craig commented.

'Yeah, the way it keeps coming back, it's almost like that boto is trying to tell us something,' Brittany remarked.

Jody caught her breath. Of course! The boto's increasingly desperate movements had been tugging at her memory, and now she knew why. Apollo had acted like that – rushing up to the boat and then away – when he had needed their help! That time, another dolphin had been trapped.

'I think Britt may be right,' she said slowly. 'The boto seems to want our help.' Suddenly, she was sure of it. 'Oh, please, Leon – can we follow her? Something's wrong . . . if that *is* Valentine, Posy might be in trouble!'

Leon nodded, pulling on the tiller to change their direction.

It was clear that the boto did want them to follow, for she stayed with them.

Leon powered down the motor so they were

Valentine leads the way . . .

travelling more slowly, explaining, 'I've never seen a boto keep up such a speed for so long – I don't want to exhaust her!'

Jody chewed her lip anxiously. She wished they could go faster, yet she knew that what Leon said made sense. If they wanted to follow Valentine they would have to keep down to her speed.

'I don't like the look of this,' Leon said in a low voice.

'What's wrong?' Craig asked him.

Leon gestured at the river. 'Low water . . . see that sandbank ahead? We can't go much farther in this direction. Too dangerous. We could get stuck.'

Jody shielded her eyes against the sun and gazed out at the ridge of muddy ground poking out like an island in the middle of the river. It loomed up, getting closer.

Leon let the engine idle while considering what to do next.

'Valentine's heading straight for the sandbank!' Jody cried, watching the boto surge past.

'Good fishing,' Leon explained. 'Fish get stuck out of water, and the botos come along and scoop them up, no problem.' He shook his head. 'But we can't follow her any farther. No, I think we'd better turn back.'

Jody stared at the boto who was swimming anxiously back and forth near the sandbank. She didn't seem to have fishing on her mind.

Then, as she raised her eyes to the sandbank, Jody caught her breath. For the first time she realised that it wasn't just a bare, empty stretch of muddy river bottom. There was something lying on it, out of the water. It was a greyish colour, so that at first it had blended in with the sandbank. But it was moving.

'Posy!' Juan gasped. He'd recognised the form of the dolphin calf a split second before Jody.

Leon frowned. 'Are you sure?'

'Yes!' Jody cried. 'That's Valentine's calf! She's stuck on the sandbank!'

'Oh, no!' gasped Brittany. She came over to sit beside Juan and peer out at the stranded boto calf. 'Oh, we have to save her!'

They all looked at Leon. His expression was grim. 'I wish we could,' he said. 'But I don't see how. For a start, I'd have to bring the boat much closer, and risk us all getting stuck . . .'

'Couldn't one of us wade over there and just lift Posy to safety?' Craig asked. 'I volunteer. I'd be very gentle with her, and I wouldn't have to carry her very far. I reckon I could do it.'

'What about the piranhas?' Brittany asked anxiously. 'Remember what happened when I put my hand in the water!'

Craig smiled at her. 'I'm willing to risk it,' he said. 'I've got my boots on, and I'm a pretty fast mover.'

'No, it's far too dangerous,' Leon said firmly. 'I can't let you go.'

Craig frowned, puzzled. 'But why not?'

'You don't understand,' Leon replied. He gestured at the sandbank. 'I know this area. That is not ordinary mud – it's very treacherous, what we call "sinking sand". If you step into it, every movement will pull you deeper down. And the heavier the object, the quicker it sinks. That's why I'm so worried about the boat. Normally, if I run her aground it's easy enough to push her out into the water again. But here . . . we could get completely bogged down and never get out.' He shook his head. 'Craig, you're a big, strong man. You could carry the calf yourself – but her weight, plus yours, would sink you. It's far too dangerous.'

Sadly, he concluded, 'This is a very painful decision, believe me. I hate to abandon Posy, but I don't see any way we can safely approach . . .'

'But she'll die if we can't save her!' Jody burst out. 'There must be a way!'

'I can do it,' Juan said suddenly, a determined look on his face. 'Leon, listen to me, *por favor*. My friends and I have done this before – we make a sort of bridge and we can get across the dangerous sands without sinking. Maybe it wouldn't work for you or

Dr McGrath, but I don't weigh so much.'

Leon nodded thoughtfully. 'You could be right,' he began, but then his face fell. He shook his head. 'I think we could get you out to Posy, Juan, but there's no way you could lift her to carry her to safety. She's only a baby, but she'll weigh more than forty kilos already. That's more than you weigh, *hijo*.'

'I could help,' Jody said eagerly. 'I'm no heavier than Juan. If we worked together . . . if we had something to carry Posy in, like a stretcher, I'm sure we could do it!'

'Oh, Jody, no!' Gina cried out, shaking her head. 'That sounds far too dangerous!'

Jody stared at her mother in dismay. 'But, Mom, Juan can't do it on his own. I have to help him! If we don't rescue Posy, she'll *die!*'

'There must be some other way,' Gina said. 'Let's give this some careful thought, and go back to the station for equipment–'

'There's no time for that, I'm afraid,' Leon interrupted. 'Jody is right. Posy is probably weak already, from struggling to get back to the water. The day is getting hotter. The longer she is out in the hot sun, the less likely she is to survive. If we can't do something right away, we might as well forget about it.'

'I'm sorry,' Gina said quietly. 'But I won't let Jody risk her life.'

Jody opened her mouth to protest.

But before she could say anything, Juan moved close to Gina and spoke to her urgently. '*Señora* McGrath,' he said, 'I tell you, I have done this many times. There is truly no danger if the patch of sinking sand is not too big, and we can make a bridge across it. I promise, I will look after Jody. She will be safe with me.'

'And if either of them looks like getting into any trouble, we can throw them a rope and haul them to safety,' Craig put in.

Hearing her father say that, Jody knew she had won.

Gina nodded, accepting it. She bit her lip and looked at Leon. 'Do you really think this will work?'

'I don't know,' Leon replied honestly. 'But we have to try.' He started up the motor and guided the boat slowly and carefully towards the sandbank. 'We're Posy's only hope of survival.'

10

Keeping a keen eye on the river, Leon motored slowly ahead, bringing the boat as close to the sandbar as he dared. Then he switched off the motor and stood up. 'These seats will do for the planks,' he said. 'Craig, would you give me a hand taking them apart? There's some tools in that box.'

The two men swiftly set about taking apart the inside of the boat.

'We need to make some sort of a sling for Posy,' Gina said. 'I wonder if there's anything useful in one of these lockers? Help me look, please, girls.'

Brittany found a large, blue, waterproof poncho.

'That'll do,' Gina decided, casting a critical eye over it. She got her miniature sewing kit from her hold-all, and perched on one of the remaining seats as she turned the poncho into a sling.

Jody looked at Juan. He was staring across to the calf on the sandbank. 'Is she still OK?' she asked him anxiously.

'I think so,' Juan replied. 'She's very still . . . I think she is worn out. But that's not bad for us, if she is too tired to struggle when we try to help her. And I think it must be firm sand over there – she isn't sinking.'

'How will we move her?' Jody asked. 'Will we try to get her into the sling and then pull her across the sand to the water?'

'No, don't pull her over the ground,' Leon said. He paused, setting the planks from the seats to one side, and wiped his face with a handkerchief. 'You might hurt her. Carrying her would be better. I think we can rig up a sort of carrying pole with this,' he added.

Bending down to where the tools were kept, he came up with a long, light aluminium pole with a hook on the end. It was normally used for pushing the boat away from docks, or snagging things floating past in the water. He turned with it towards Gina to ask, 'Could you fasten the sling to this?'

Gina nodded, only glancing briefly up from her work of cutting and stitching.

Leon frowned worriedly at Juan and Jody. 'You know, forty or fifty kilos is awfully heavy . . . I really don't think you could make it safely across sinking sand supporting such a weight.'

'We won't have to,' said Juan, sounding confident. 'I think there's solid ground on the other side of the sandbank, and the sinking sand is only on this side.'

'Maybe we should move the boat,' Craig suggested.

But Leon shook his head. 'It's too risky. This is a safer position for the boat. I hope Juan is right about the sinking sand . . .' He looked inquiringly at the boy. 'Do you know how to recognise patches of sinking sand?'

Juan nodded. 'Yes. I'll be careful, don't worry! I'll tell Jody where to step. We'll save Posy.'

He sounded absolutely certain, Jody thought. She wished she felt the same! But she had butterflies in her stomach . . . in fact, she was terrified. But if her parents knew how scared she was they might not let her go, she thought.

'Let's get a walkway into place,' Leon said, grasping one of the boards with both hands.

While Leon and Craig lowered the first two planks into the sand, Juan inspected Jody. 'Take your shoes off,' he advised. 'It's easier in bare feet.'

Jody quickly took off her trainers and socks.

'OK,' said Craig, looking around at Jody and Juan. 'Now you kids will have to check that these will bear your weight, and, if they will, then put the next two into place.'

'It'll be like building your own road as you go,' Leon added. 'If you get into trouble, we'll throw you this.' He displayed a length of rope. 'Should worse come to worst, we can pull you to safety.'

Jody's stomach clenched with fear. She couldn't help imagining herself caught and sucked down by the treacherous sinking sands. For a moment, she was frozen, unable to move.

'Come,' said Juan urgently to Jody. 'We'll be OK – and we must get to Posy, quickly!'

Jody gulped back her fear and nodded. She had to concentrate on saving Posy.

Her dad kissed her. Then Gina came forward

to give them the sling and carrying-pole. She hugged Jody tightly. 'Be careful, sweetheart,' she murmured.

Jody gave her a tremulous smile. Then she followed Juan over the side of the boat and onto the planks.

At first it seemed all right. Craig and Leon passed the other planks across to Juan and Jody, who each carried one. But when they got to the end of the first 'walkway' and paused to put down the next plank, there was an ominous slurping sound. Mud bubbled up around the edges of the plank, pulling at it.

Jody felt herself sinking, and cried out in fright.

'Keep going!' Juan said urgently. 'Just keep moving!'

Jody wobbled, nearly fell, then managed to lurch across onto the next plank, her heart pounding.

She looked ahead to where Posy was resting in a few centimetres of water. The boto calf was lying very still, but now Jody was close enough to see her blowhole puckering open and shut as she breathed. Although streaked with sand from her struggles, Posy looked very pink, almost as brightly coloured as her mother.

'She's scared,' Juan said softly. 'But she's going to be OK.'

As they approached Posy, Juan began to speak to her in Spanish, his voice low and gentle.

Jody hoped that Posy remembered him and that his familiar presence would make her feel better.

'OK, now, let's get Posy into her carrier,' he said, crouching down beside the calf. The ground here was quite firm. Although their bare feet sank a little into the soft, squishy mud, there was no danger. Posy might be stuck, but that was only because she wasn't strong enough to wriggle her way into deeper water – she was certainly not sinking.

Jody crouched down and put her arms around Posy. The boto's skin was smooth, soft and very warm. She felt the calf tense with alarm, and heard a high-pitched squealing sound. 'Sssh, sssh, baby, it's OK,' Jody murmured gently as she struggled to lift her. Posy was much heavier – and bigger – than she had expected.

Working together, she and Juan just managed to raise her up and slip the makeshift sling snugly around her body. Jody knew that neither one of them could have managed on their own.

Jody was pouring with sweat by the time they'd made Posy secure. The calf had stopped squealing by then and was no longer struggling. Jody hoped she realised that she and Juan were only trying to help her. 'Which way should we go?' she asked Juan.

He peered at the sand around them, then gave a satisfied nod. 'There's no sinking sand on this side at all. We'll go that way,' he said, pointing. 'You can see the marks . . . that was where Valentine and Posy came out of the water . . . and where Valentine went back again. It will be the shortest way back to the water, and the safest.'

Jody nodded. She took a deep breath and grasped one end of the pole.

Juan did the same. 'Ready?' he asked.

Jody nodded, and together, they raised the pole, slowly lifting Posy away from the ground. She was a heavy burden, but, with the two of them, would not be too much to carry, Jody thought, relieved.

Then Posy gave a wriggle. Flexing her tail, she seemed to be trying to swim away through the air!

Jody gasped, thrown off-balance as the burden lurched wildly. She settled her heels firmly and managed not to fall. 'Oh, please be still, Posy!' she begged.

'*Calmate*,' murmured Juan.

Juan led and Jody followed, trying to keep her end of the pole as steady and level as she could. It could be a disaster if Posy made them overbalance, or if she managed to wriggle out of the sling and landed heavily on the ground, with no cushioning water to break her fall.

Jody gritted her teeth and hung on to the pole grimly. She longed to go faster, to break into a run, to get this dangerous journey over with – but Juan was being cautious, inspecting every patch of ground for signs that it might hide a patch of the treacherous sinking sand.

Deeper water was no more than six or seven metres away, but it felt to Jody like the longest journey she had ever taken. Her back and shoulder muscles ached from the strain of supporting the wriggling boto. Her heart lurched and her stomach twisted every time her feet sank in the mud, fearful that they would encounter another patch of sinking sand. Sweat poured into her eyes, stinging them, and the breath rasped in her throat.

And then, after a seemingly endless struggle, she felt cool water splash beneath her feet. Another step brought the water to her knees. Then she was thigh-deep, and another dolphin – Valentine – was blowing to the surface right beside them.

As gently as they could, Jody and Juan lowered Posy into the water. With fumbling fingers, Jody unfastened the sling from the pole and pulled it carefully away from Posy, who was now flexing and wriggling madly, showering them both with muddy water in her excitement.

As soon as she was free, the calf darted forward, on a collision course with her mother, who immediately guided her away.

'She's all right!' Jody exclaimed. She felt weak with relief, yet also drained. Her legs were trembling.

'Yes, she is safe with her mother now,' Juan agreed. He rested one hand on Jody's shoulder. 'We did it. Come, let's get back to the boat.'

November 13 – Siesta time.
I can't believe this is our last full day at the research station. We've had such a great time. Tonight, we're invited to Juan's village for a fiesta. (That's a big party!)

The kids at his school have made up a play which they are going to perform. Juan is being very mysterious about it, but I've guessed that it is about dolphins.

Saw Posy and Valentine again today. Posy seems absolutely fine, no bad effects from her stranding. I think Valentine has finally learned her lesson, after nearly losing her baby, and will look after Posy much more carefully from now on!

Ocho is as mischievous as ever – he nearly turned the boat over this morning! – but at least he's keeping close to his mom!

Everyone from the research centre went along to Juan's village that evening, a couple of them squeezed on board the *Tonina*.

The old river wooden boat still showed signs of the recent adventure. Although Leon and Carlos had hammered the seats back into place, one or two were still slightly wonky.

Juan was waiting by the dock to meet them. He looked anxious.

'Brittany, I have a great favour to ask you,' he blurted out. 'One of the girls is ill and can't be in our play. It's the most important part! Would you take her place?'

Brittany looked taken aback. 'How could I? There's no time for me to learn a part for tonight!' she objected.

'There are only two short lines to say,' Juan told her. 'You speak Spanish so beautifully . . . I am sure you could remember two lines. And you would be perfect!'

Brittany hesitated, then shook her head. 'No, I couldn't. I'm sure I wouldn't be any good. You'd better find somebody else,' she murmured.

Jody could hardly believe her ears. Brittany had told her about being in her school play last year, and her dreams of being a model or an actress some day. Surely she wasn't afraid . . .

'But there is nobody else!' Juan exclaimed. 'Oh, please!'

'Well . . .' Brittany said slowly. 'I'm not sure . . .' She paused dramatically, gazing expectantly at Juan.

'Get Jody to do it,' Jimmy piped up.

Juan turned to her. 'Would you?'

Jody swallowed hard. She didn't really want to, but she wouldn't let Juan down.

'Well, I guess I could,' she began.

'Jody! Her Spanish is rotten – she'd get the lines wrong – I'd do a much better job!' Brittany burst out, without thinking.

'Why don't you, then?' Jody said. She grinned – Brittany had only wanted to be coaxed. 'Of course, if you really don't want to . . .'

Brittany tossed her long, fair hair back, and sighed. 'Oh, well, I guess I'd better.'

Juan grinned. 'Thank you! You will be wonderful! The play will be wonderful! Come with me; we'll tell my teacher, and you'll learn your lines.'

The play was performed in the village school.

Jody, Jimmy, Sean, and their parents, along with Dr Taylor, Leon, Julie, Carlos and at least fifty villagers crowded into the building. The single large classroom had been cleared of desks and chairs to make room for them all.

Jody looked around at the walls. One was covered with a large painted mural of a river and a riverbank. The others were decorated by many small, brightly-painted pictures of animals, birds, fish and fruit.

'Those are bark paintings,' Julie explained,

noticing Jody's interest. 'They're a traditional local art form.'

Soon, everyone was seated on the floor. Conversation died away as the teacher, Señor Molinas, came out and stood in front of them, waiting for silence.

When he had their attention, Señor Miercoles began to speak. Julie whispered a translation in Jody's ear as her parents did the same for the twins.

The teacher explained that the play was based on local legends about the boto and that the children had written it themselves. The title was 'Botos Bring Good Fortune'.

After Sr Miercoles sat down, the play began.

A girl wearing a pink dress, her head covered by a long-nosed dolphin mask, danced about while Juan gazed at her. He said that he loved nothing better than to spend his time watching the botos in the river. Other villagers came on the scene then and made fun of Juan for wasting his time. Others cried that botos were greedy devils who stole their fish. Life would be better without them!

In the next scene, Brittany came on wearing a

white dress. Her long golden hair glowed in the dim light. Jody caught her breath in astonishment. It was easy to believe that she was magical.

Brittany spoke, inviting Juan to visit her home. As he agreed, she took his hand, and two children rushed forward to change the backdrop. Now, instead of a picture of a riverbank, there was a scene of a magical, underwater city. Juan wandered around in amazement, meeting people wearing stingray hats, armoured catfish shoes, and snake-belts. He was given the same clothes and made an honorary citizen, but decided to return to his own people. The dolphins promised that if he ever needed them they'd come to him. Brittany gave him a magic whistle.

Back on the riverbank, Juan met two scientists, who told him they had come to study the boto. At this, there was much laughter and muttering in the audience. People craned around to grin at the real scientists sitting among them.

But no one in the village could tell them anything about botos, so they had decided to leave and go somewhere else.

Juan blew his magic whistle. A line of children

wearing pink T-shirts and dolphin head masks, came dancing out.

The scientists, amazed and delighted, decided to stay. They promised that more people would come, bringing prosperity to the village of the dolphins.

The play ended with Juan a local hero, and everyone dancing.

Everyone applauded and cheered with noisy approval. Watching Brittany, smiling and flushed as she took her bows with Juan and the others, Jody thought that she had never seen the other girl look happier.

Afterwards there was a feast. Torches and fires turned night to day. Fish, chicken and vegetables were grilled on dozens of fires, sending a delicious, smoky aroma into the air. Wherever Jody went she found people smiling at her and offering her something to eat or drink.

Music started up. People played flutes, guitars and drums. Later, a more formal band set up, and a space was cleared for dancing.

The fiesta was still in full swing when Leon suggested it was time to leave. 'It won't stop until dawn,' Julie told them as they boarded *Tonina*. 'The people around here really know how to party!'

The moon was high and bright, lighting them on their way down the river.

'What a magical night,' Gina murmured. She held Craig's hand, and they both gazed out at the dark, glittering water. 'I could almost believe in that underwater city . . .'

'Sounds to me like the botos have bewitched my utterly scientific wife!' Craig said with a laugh.

Jody smiled. She leaned out over the water. Then, like the granting of her wish, a soft, sighing sound arose from the water, and she just glimpsed the sleek, rounded melon of a boto's head.

Impulsively, Jody whistled. She was longing to communicate with them, and although she'd never heard the botos vocalising in the air the way marine dolphins often did, it was the only thing she could think to do.

To her surprise, the boto swimming alongside the boat responded with a sudden burst of bubbles, silvery in the moonlight.

Or was it just coincidence?

To check it out, Jody whistled again.

Chatting with the boto . . .

A trail of silver bubbles was the response. Then the boto surfaced, breathing with the distinctive little coughing sigh that had become such a familiar and well-loved sound over the past few days.

Another whistle, and more bubbles.

The magical exchange went on for a few more minutes. Then, perhaps, the boto grew tired, trying to keep up with the boat, and vanished in the dark water.

November 14 – 5 a.m.
It's pitch dark outside. I feel like I hardly got to sleep before Mom was shaking me and telling me to get up . . . The others are having a bite to eat, but my stomach hasn't woken up yet. I've just been to pat Buddy one last time and tell him goodbye. I wish I could do the same to the dolphins – especially Ocho, Valentine and Posy!

Just then, Juan arrived.

'I've just come to say goodbye,' he said. 'I wanted to tell you how much I have enjoyed getting to know you all, and . . .' he paused, ducked his head rather shyly, then suddenly thrust something into Brittany's hand. 'I made that for you, to remember me by,' he mumbled.

Jody saw that it was a small bark painting of a boto, beautifully painted in the traditional style.

Brittany looked stunned. 'Oh, Juan – how sweet of you! It's beautiful!' she gasped. Then she bit her lip, her smile fading. 'Oh, I feel awful! I don't have anything to give you!'

'That doesn't matter,' Juan said swiftly. 'Please, don't feel bad . . . I don't need anything to remember you by.'

'How about a photo?' suggested Julie. She was holding up a Polaroid camera. 'I can take a shot of Brittany, and you can have it straight away!'

Juan brightened. 'Could I really? A picture of Brittany – to keep?' His smile was dazzling.

'Sure,' said Julie. 'Stand right there, Brittany, and look this way . . .'

'Wait, wait!' Brittany looked flustered. Her hands flew to her hair. 'I need a brush . . .'

'You look fine,' Jody assured her.

'Say "cheese" ' said Julie.

Leon hurried them through their goodbyes, and a

few minutes later the McGraths, Brittany and Dr Taylor were back on board *Tonina*. As Leon steered the boat away from the dock, and down the channel towards the main river, Jody looked back. She waved at Julie, Carlos and Juan until they were out of sight. Then she turned her attention to the river ahead.

November 14 – still morning – Orinoco River
There is so much to see and learn about life in the rainforest that I wish we could stay longer . . . but on the other hand, I am really looking forward to getting back to Dolphin Dreamer *– to see Maddie, Harry, Cam and Mei Lin again. And being back on the ocean, away from this awful heat. I can't wait to be able to stand out on the deck with the spray of salt on my face and my hair flying in the breeze as we're racing the wind again . . .*

A familiar, soft sighing sound caught Jody's attention, breaking into her thoughts.

She looked up from her diary and caught her breath as she saw several botos in the water. It was the largest group she'd seen yet. They were diving and surfacing all around the boat.

Leon cut the engine. At once, the splash of water and the gentle coughing sound of the botos' breathing filled the air around them.

Two dolphins came swimming up close to Jody's side of the boat. She leaned over to get a good look at them. They responded by rising up in the water. The bigger one was a very bright pink. The smaller one was just a baby.

'Valentine! Posy!' Jody cried out happily as she recognised them.

The two botos, mother and calf, gazed up at Jody with their bright eyes, and nodded their heads.

'Goodbye,' Jody murmured. Her eyes stung with happy tears as she watched them dive down and swim around the boat. 'Goodbye, and good luck!'

You will find lots more about dolphins on these websites:

The Whale and Dolphin Conservation Society
www.wdcs.org

International Dolphin Watch
www.idw.org